RIO DESPERADO

When Burke Dane set out to avenge the lynching of his half-brother he never figured on becoming a hunted man himself.

Books by Gordon D. Shirreffs
in the Linford Western Library:

THE VALIANT BUGLES
SHOWDOWN IN SONORA
SOUTHWEST DRIFTER
SHADOW VALLEY
TOP GUN
AMBUSH ON THE MESA
BUGLES ON THE PRAIRIE
FORT VENGEANCE
BOWMAN'S KID
BRASADA
TRAIL'S END
THE GODLESS BREED
FIVE GRAVES TO BOOT HILL
RIO DIABLO
JACK OF SPADES
NOW HE IS LEGEND
CODE OF THE GUN
MANHUNTER
RENEGADE'S TRAIL
RIDE A LONE TRAIL
HANGIN' PARDS
TUMBLEWEED TRIGGER
RENEGADE LAWMAN
SHADOW OF A GUNMAN
GUNSLINGERS THREE
APACHE BUTTE
THE HIDDEN RIDER OF DARK MOUNTAIN
RIO DESPERADO

GORDON D. SHIRREFFS

RIO DESPERADO

Complete and Unabridged

LINFORD
Leicester

First Linford Edition
published January 1990

British Library CIP Data

Shirreffs, Gordon D. (Gordon Donald)
   Rio desperado.—Large print ed.—
   Linford western library
   I. Title
   813'.54[F]

   ISBN 0-7089-6800-7

Published by
F. A. Thorpe (Publishing) Ltd.
Anstey, Leicestershire
Set by Rowland Phototypesetting Ltd.
Bury St. Edmunds, Suffolk
Printed and bound in Great Britain by
T. J. Press (Padstow) Ltd., Padstow, Cornwall

1

THE gaunt, wind-tortured tree at the top of the pass bore strange and gruesome fruit. Burke Dane slid from his saddle and walked toward the tree. Behind him, down a long and twisted road, was the valley of the Little Bonito, fully concealed by the low hanging mists of that cold and rainy day. Beyond the pass, hidden from sight by more mist, was the valley of the Rio Desperado. To certain men, the top of the pass was the point of no return. To the bluefaced man whose body hung in the whining wind of those heights it had been the end of the trail.

Burke stopped ten feet from the lynched man and slowly rolled a cigarette. There was no expression on his lean and angular face. The blue eyes were as hard as glacier ice. He read the crudely lettered placard that had been fastened to the soaked cowhide vest of the dead man. "Rustler," said Burke Dane in a low voice. He spat to one side before he lighted his cigarette. His lips drew back to one side as he looked down toward the misty valley of the Rio Desperado. Then he looked back at the hanging man. "Charley," he said quietly, "I've come to take you home."

There was no haste as Burke cut down the stiffened corpse and placed it on a flat slab of rock. He worked the taut noose loose from the deep groove it had dug into the cold flesh. He made no attempt to straighten the grotesquely crooked neck and head. He bound the body first in a blanket and then in a rectangle of tarpaulin and carried it to the big dun. The dun shied and blowed as Burke placed the corpse across the saddle and lashed it in place.

Burke walked back to the tree and picked up the rope. It was a fine reata, handmade as far as he could tell, and braided by an expert. Four-stranded and made of rawhide. An expensive rope for a vaquero to buy. Most of them carried a *grass* rope made of Manila hemp. Burke slowly coiled the rope and carried it back to the dun. He led the big horse back down the trail toward the valley of the Little Bonito.

The rain began to beat down on his slicker and on the tarpaulin that covered and protected the lynched body of Charley Mayo—younger half brother of Burke Dane.

The ranch land spread along both sides of the Big Bonito as far as the eye could see. The log buildings were well built, though not large. They were designed to be practical as well as beautiful. Charley Mayo's tastes had always revealed his two prime characteristics of businesslike workmanship and love of the beautiful country in which he was born and raised. No man could have selected a better place in the Territory of New Mexico to build a ranch and a future.

It was just turning dusk as Burke Dane's dun clattered across the log bridge that spanned the rushing river. He tugged at the halter rope of the stray burro he had roped in the valley of the Little Bonito, miles to the west, to carry the body of Charley Mayo home to its final resting place. The rain that had been holding off all day continued to patter down, dappling the dark waters of the Big Bonito and slanting in leaden colored veils down through the tops of the forest clearings to further soak the wet ground.

Through the rain, the yellow lighted windows of the ranch house appeared. A thread of smoke rose from the big field-stone chimney, only to be beaten down by the cold rain. The wind shifted and with it came the tempting odor of roasting meat. Hungry as Burke Dane was, for he had not eaten all that day, the thought of food did not appeal to him. He took the wet cigarette butt from his tight lips and flipped it into the water.

He led the dun to the side of the corral and ground-reined it. He walked back to the burro and its bundled burden, and for the first time since he had found his

4

brother, a trace of wetness showed in the hard blue eyes. It was not grief for Charley, that was already buried deep— though not forgotten, within the lean body of Burke Dane; it was grief for the young woman in the house, and for her little brood. The young woman who had sent a message to El Paso to find the older half brother of Charley, so that he would look for his missing brother. It was the one thing that could have brought Burke back to the country of the Big Bonito.

Burke shook his head. He led the burro to a lean-to, took off the soaked tarpaulin and its contents. He placed the body atop a pile of hay and felt for the makings. Then he stopped. There was no use in stalling. He'd have to face Marion with the truth. He walked toward the house and onto the wide front porch that had such a pleasing vista of the valley and the river. Burke heard her voice in the kitchen. He closed his eyes and prayed for strength. He had not prayed for anything in years, for Burke Dane, by thought and deed, was hardly a man of God.

Burke slammed a hard fist sideways against the wet door, then peeled off his slicker. Feet pattered on the puncheon floor and the door swung open to emit a flood of warm light and the mingled odors of a finely cooked meal. A small girl stood there looking up at the big man whose face was shaded by the brim of his hat. The little lady smiled and ran forward to wrap her tiny arms about his knees. "Mama!" she screamed. "It's Uncle Burke!"

A dish clattered to the kitchen floor and Burke heard the sound of hurried footsteps. In a moment she was there, framed in the kitchen doorway, wiping her slim hands on her apron while she looked eagerly at Burke.

"Burke!" she said, "You found him?"

He opened his mouth and then shut it.

"Burke?" She came forward into the room, tucking away a stray wisp of her lovely brown hair. Her gray eyes searching his weathered and bristly face.

"Burke?" Her voice faltered a little. "Did you find him?"

He nodded. "I found him, Marion," he said at last. He gently disengaged little Dolly's arms from his legs and led her toward her mother. He kicked the door shut behind him. "He's outside in the lean-to," he said quickly, for want of anything better to say.

She eyed him closely and then she knew. "How did it happen, Burke?" she asked in a low voice.

He reached out an awkward hand and rested it on her shoulder. "Now, Marion," he said gently.

"Tell me!" she insisted.

He looked down at the little girl.

"She doesn't understand, Burke," said Marion.

Burke looked at Marion. Without a word he took the soggy placard from within his coat and held it out to her. She stared at the almost illegible word written on it, then at Burke.

"I don't understand," she said quietly.

7

Then her eyes widened. "Not that, Burke! Not *that!*" she almost screamed.

He nodded and looked away from her. "I found him at the top of Windy Pass," he said. "Right beside the trail. He was there several days at least." He caught her swiftly as she fell.

"Mama asleep, Uncle Burke?" asked little Dolly.

"Mama asleep," said Burke mechanically as he carried her to her room. He covered her with a quilt, then closed the door behind him. He hurried to the kitchen and inspected the meal, doing what had to be done. He knew then and there that she had expected the both of them, for the meal was one of Charley's favorites, and on top of the stove shelf were three berry pies, all favorites of Burke Dane. He walked into the living room and peeled off his damp coat. Dolly came to him and he picked her up, then walked to place his back against the fireplace to feel the grateful drying heat of the fire.

A door creaked open and Print

Campbell, Marion's father stood there, staring unseeingly toward Burke. "That you, Charley?" he asked.

"It's Burke Dane, Print," said Burke quietly.

A strange look fled across the sightless face. "Where's Charley?"

"Charley is dead, Print."

The wall clock ticked along and then Print spoke again. "How did it happen?"

"They lynched him atop Windy Pass, Print. Some days ago, from the looks of him."

"Who did it, Burke?"

"*Quien sabe?*"

Print felt his way to a chair and sat down heavily. "I told him to stay out of the Rio Desperado country, Burke. He wouldn't listen. You know how he was, Burke."

"Yes."

"Leastways he could have taken some of his own boys with him. No! He had to hire men over in that hellhole. Charley thought a lot of his ability to take care of himself, Burke."

"It runs in the family, Print."

The strange look fled across the face again. "Yeh. But Charley was a good man, Burke. Don't you misunderstand me. He took care of me, Burke." Print passed a hand across his sightless eyes. "You'd have thought *this* would have warned him to stay away from that damned Rio Desperado country."

Burke looked away although he knew the old man could not see him. Print Campbell had lost his sight in the Rio Desperado country years ago and had almost lost his life along with it. A load of birdshot at close range had done the job. Print Campbell, so the story goes, knew too much about certain men. Not only did the incident close his eyes forever, but it sealed his lips as well, for if Print Campbell talked, quite a few men, still riding free and easy in the Rio Desperado country would have long since had the same fate as that of Charley Mayo. Although they would have had the benefit of law and a trial to boot.

Footsteps sounded in the hallway and

Marion Mayo came into the room. Her eyes were red and swollen but her voice was steady as she spoke.

"You're cold, wet and hungry, Burke. Change your clothes. Some of Charley's things will fit you. By the time you've changed, supper will be on the table. Father, take care of Dolly. The baby is asleep, Burke. You can see him when he wakes up."

Burke handed Dolly to her grandfather. He nodded. It was the way of the women of that country. Marion Campbell had filled the gap in Charley Mayo's life seven years ago. She had satisfied his two prime characteristics. She was a practical and beautiful woman; a fine wife and a loving mother. Now Charley was gone, never to return to this earth, and her other menfolk needed to be fed and taken care of in the best way she knew how. It was as simple as that.

Burke went hesitantly into the bedroom. The lamp was lit and the quilt was neatly folded and placed at the foot of the bed. Marion Mayo's grief was oceans deep, but her discipline would carry her through in safety.

Burke swiftly changed his clothes. He carried his wet things into the kitchen to dry and hung his damp gunbelt behind the stove to slowly dry out. He withdrew his Colt, emptied it, wiped it carefully, tested the action, then placed it on a shelf. It wasn't until he was done with that automatic task that he realized that both Marion and her father were looking at him. They had heard the spinning of the cylinder, the crisp metallic clicking of the hand-honed action. His face hardened a little. Neither of them had ever believed in gunplay, at least the sort Burke Dane was known to practice.

Marion silently served them, then turned away from the table. "There are more biscuits in the warming oven," she said. She reached for her rain cape.

"No," said Burke quickly. He stood up from the table. His knife dropped to the floor.

She smiled gently. "I'll have to see him sometime, Burke," she said.

He passed a hand across his face. "Well, that is, I don't know *what* to say."

She walked to the kitchen door. "I'll be all right," she said.

He withdrew his clasp knife and walked to her. "The lashings are wet. Cut them," he said. He took a lantern from the shelf beside the door and lighted it for her. She took it silently and walked into the darkness. He watched her cross to the lean-to through the pattering rain and a great sickness came up within him. He walked back to the table.

"You couldn't stop her," said Print quietly.

"No."

The blind man shoved back his plate. "Can't hardly eat, Burke. I was only eatin' to please her."

"Me too. Smoke?"

"Please."

Burke rolled two cigarettes, placed one in the old man's mouth and lighted it. "She's lovelier than ever, Print," he said. "Breaks a man's heart to look at her."

Print blew out a mouthful of smoke. "You still love her, Burke?"

"I'd rather not talk about it, Print."

The old man leaned forward and looked directly at Burke, almost as though he could really see him. "Maybe we got to talk about it, Burke. She's got no one but me now and I ain't no use to her. She's got those two kids to take care of. She can't run this ranch, man! *You* can."

"Just what are you driving at?"

Print took the cigarette from his dry lips. "You're all she's got now to take care of her, Burke."

"Hell of a time to talk about that now!"

"Maybe Charley would have wanted it that way."

"Yeh," said Burke dryly. "You and Marion, and Charley. Maybe that time was seven years ago, Print. You know damned well why I left the Big Bonito country, man."

Print shrugged. "It was your decision. Charley was still here. He was a lot like you, Burke. She was lonely. Charley was good to her."

"She loved him, didn't she?"

A piece of firewood snapped in the big range. The rain slashed suddenly against the misted windows. Little Dolly scraped her plate and looked curiously at the two big men on each side of her. The wind moaned down the chimney.

"Yes," said the old man at last. "She *grew* to love him I think, Burke. It wasn't hard." He stared sightlessly at Burke. "But she never forgot *you*, Burke."

Burke got up and rolled another cigarette. He laughed dryly. "Same old Print," he said in a hard voice. "Looking out for his own. You'd tell me that just to make damned good and sure I'd stick around and take care of my brother's wife and *his* kids. Well, I don't buy that, Print! I'm leaving here before dawn." An odd feeling fled over Burke. He turned slowly to see Marion standing in the open doorway, the rain dripping from her cape. She was looking directly at him with her lovely and tragic eyes. *How much had she heard?*

She put out the lantern, removed her

15

cape and hung it up, closed the door and crossed to the stove. "Hot berry pie for dessert," she said quietly.

Burke's face tightened. Damn the old man and his ways! Seven years ago he had made it well known he wanted no part of Burke Dane as a son-in-law and in those days Print Campbell's word was pretty near law in the valley of the Big Bonito. That was before he had found a tougher law in the valley of the Rio Desperado and had paid for it with his sight.

"I'll take Charley into the spare room," said Burke. He walked into the living room and got his slicker. He left the house and stomped across to the lean-to. He picked up the body of his brother and carried it back to the house, shielding the blue face from the rain with his hat. He took the body in the back way and into the little spare room at the rear of the house. He placed it on the bed in the darkness and closed the door behind him.

They were waiting for him in the living room. Marion and her father, with little Dolly playing on the floor, and the baby

16

boy, Alan, cradled in his grandfather's arms. "I'll be leaving before dawn, as I said," spoke Burke as he lighted a cigarette.

"Back to El Paso?" asked Print tonelessly.

"No, Print. Back over Windy Pass and into Arizona Territory."

"But that's the Rio Desperado country!" said Marion. Her hand crept up to her throat.

Burke nodded.

"But why?" asked Marion.

Burke leaned against the fireplace. "My brother went over there to buy cattle. You said at supper he was carrying a thousand dollars with him for that purpose. Charley didn't get the cattle and the money is gone. Charley was murdered. I'm going back to get the man, or *men* who did the job, and I'm bringing back the cattle or the money for you, Marion."

She stood up and slowly shook her head. "They'll kill you too!"

Burke shrugged. "They can try. I don't think anyone over there knows I am

17

Charley's brother. I haven't been around here for seven years. I think I've changed considerably in those seven years, haven't I?"

There was no need for them to answer, the answer was plain on their faces.

"This is no time for that," said Print slowly. His face hardened. "You've got to show respect for your dead brother, Burke. Aren't you going to stay for the funeral?"

"The best respect I can show for Charley is to do exactly what I said I intend to do."

"It ain't right!" snapped Print. "You're going to stay here until Charley is properly buried! You hear me?"

Burke looked at Marion. "I can't stay here, Marion," he said. "No one knows I'm back in this country. If I stay for the funeral and word gets around who I am, my chances of running down his murderers will be gone when I reach the top of Windy Pass." He smiled crookedly. "I might end up the way Charley did."

"I understand that," she said quietly. "But I don't understand why you have to go. It isn't worth it, Burke. Not to me, it isn't."

He straightened up. "It is to *me*," he said. "I've got to go, Marion."

"Damned fool!" snapped Print Campbell.

Burke eyed him. "It's said you know a lot more about those people over there than anyone around here, Print."

"I don't know anything!"

"Yes you do," said Marion. She looked at her father. "You'll have to tell him, Father."

Print's face worked. "All right," he said at last. "It really doesn't matter anymore. I'm old and helpless now. A burden on you, Marion."

"I didn't mean it that way," she said quickly.

"I know." He smiled. "Well, maybe if I was all right, I'd do as Burke is going to do. I'll tell you all I can, Burke, though God alone knows if it is of any value."

The fire was almost dead, and Marion

had long ago gone to bed, when at last Print Campbell finished filling in Burke Dane with all he knew, from actual experience or from hearsay about the Rio Desperado country.

Burke stood up and stretched. He was dead weary and ready for bed. "Say goodbye to Marion for me," he said quietly. He took out his wallet and separated five one hundred dollar bills from the money within it. "Give this to Marion. She can pay me when I bring back the money Charley lost over there."

"Yeh," said Print quietly. "Thanks, Burke."

"You don't think I'll be back then?"

The old man looked up at him. "No. Do you?"

Burke put out the lamp. "I don't know, Print. I don't know. But there is one thing I am sure of: I'll ram my navel into the sand trying!"

"Amen," said Print Campbell.

The wind whipped along the valley of the Big Bonito, on its way to lonely and haunted Windy Pass, to plunge into the valley of the Rio Desperado far to west, almost gleefully, as though to spread the news that Burke Dane was on his way and that death would be a close rider of the big man from El Paso.

2

BURKE DANE, through no choice of his own, was ascending Windy Pass from the valley of the Little Bonito in the howling darkness of a wind and rain storm that had begun in the late afternoon. Lightning crackled and snapped along the rimrock, etching the fanged peaks against an eerie sky while in the canyons and through the wind-swept passes the thunder drums rolled in mad fury. There would be no shelter on the eastern side of Windy Pass that night, nor indeed within the pass itself, for the rain-laden wind swept through it as though it was a gigantic funnel lashing and bending the tortured trees and stripping them of their leaves.

He hunched within his slicker trying to light a quirly but it was no use. There would be no solace of tobacco for him until he descended the pass into the valley of the Rio Desperado. The thought of trying to camp out that night even on the more sheltered side of the mountains was hardly tempting.

The top of the pass was deep in wet darkness when he reached it at last, hoping to God he could pass through and not see the scene of his brother's horrible death, but such a break was not allowed him that night. The lightning shafted repeatedly through the streaming skies, marking the lone tree in its twisted nakedness. The memory of what he had seen there was etched on his mind no matter how hard he tried to think of other subjects.

The dun stumbled at the top of the pass and immediately began to favor a leg. Burke spat a curse into the night and slid from the saddle to examine the left fore hoof of the dun. It was then that he heard something crying eerily above the mad howling of the wind. A cold feeling swept over him as he straightened up, but he could not bring himself to look at that damned tree as though afraid of what he might see there; something not of this earth, but familiar enough to him.

The crying came again, distorted by the wind. Burke peered down the western side of the pass as the lightning flashed with almost stunning force above the peaks. There was a gap in the narrow roadway with a small area close to the mountain side where he would pass. There had been a slide and a big one. It was not there when he found Charley's body. He led the dun down the streaming roadway to stop at the gap. The lightning seared through the sky and he saw something white far below, a faint movement. Then the area was plunged again into darkness. But there had been just enough time to know that it was a man down there, clinging for dear life to a rock.

Burke stepped back from the edge and took his reata from the wet saddle. He knew it was too far for the rope to reach, so he took the gruesome relic of his brother's death from a saddlebag and linked the two reatas together. Stones and rocks slid from beneath his boots as he moved toward the edge and he threw himself backwards. A voice rose above the clattering of the fall. "Take it easy, for God's sake!"

Burke led the dun back and tethered him to a tree; made the end of the line fast to the saddlehorn, then he coiled the linked lines and held them in his left hand. The lightning gave him enough illumination to allow him to pick his way partly down the treacherous slope. It also showed him that beyond the base of the slide there was nothing except a sheer drop hundreds of feet into the wet woods below.

He hung onto the line with his right hand and eased himself down. Now and then loose rock slid from beneath his dug-in feet. Despite the cold wetness of the night he was sweating profusely. Halfway down the slope the lightning lanced through the skies to stab into a naked and towering butte on the far side of the pass. He saw then that the man was farther down than before and that his legs were dangling into space.

There was no use in trying to drop a noose over the man. There was nothing to do but inch down that treacherous slope, hoping that the sliding rock wouldn't push him over the brink, or stun him into letting go his weak hold. Further and further he descended until he was within two yards of the man. He could see the strained face, the wide eyes, the sickness within him. "Keep a mane holt!" he yelled as he shifted the coil to his right hand and the line to his left. A foot slipped and his full weight was held by the taut line.

"I'm going!" screamed the man.

Burke slid down the line. One foot went over the edge. He held the line with a grip of steel and dropped the coil, trying to get it around the man, but it slid over the edge and dangled into darkness.

"Oh God!" screamed the man.

Burke lunged and gripped a handful of wet cloth in his left hand, twisting it to get a better grip, while he hooked his left leg about the man. Rock and dirt cascaded down both sides of them and then Burke felt that the man's full weight was dangling. *If that line broke!*

He worked a leg about the man. The strain was telling on his right arm. "Grab the line, damn you!" he yelled.

The weight was dead on him now as the man gripped the line, slipped and gripped it again. "Got it!" he said.

Burke gritted his teeth. "Get a leg up," he said.

The man raised a leg and seemed to find a footing. Burke slowly and steadily dug in his left boot, hoping to God he didn't break loose, for if the weight of the man became full on his right leg breaking his grip, he knew the man would be doomed, and maybe Burke, too.

Inch by inch the man worked his way up until he could wrap his arms about Burke. His eyes were close to Burke's. "What now, *amigo?*" he said. He managed a faint grin.

Burke swallowed hard. "Ring for the operator to take us up the shaft," he said.

"Not bad." The man looked up that

steep slope. "Guess he's gone for a beer," he said.

Burke began to dig in his heels. "I'll use both hands on the line," he said. "Hang on!"

"I wasn't thinking of letting go."

It seemed to Burke Dane that they were not moving at all. It was almost as though the wet and rough surface of the earth beneath them was moving as they fought their way up, like squirrels in a turning cage. His hands were raw from contact with the wet rope and the flesh of his knees was ripped and torn by the cruel ground.

The lightning flamed coldly through the skies and thunder pealed in the gorges when, at last, Burke got a leg over the edge and threw his body over. The rescued man released his grip and rolled over and over on the rough ground until he was far from the ragged rim of the gorge. He pressed his wet face hard against the ground and his body shook spasmodically.

Burke got slowly to his feet and coiled

up the lines. He walked to the dun and rested his head against the wet leather of the saddle. He felt weak as water. He raised his head and opened a saddlebag to take out a bottle. He pulled the cork with his teeth and walked slowly back to the man whose life he had saved. He tapped him on the shoulder and handed him the bottle.

"Take a slug," he said.

"*Gracias*," The bottle was upended. The man coughed. "Jesus! That's good! Mescal?"

Burke nodded. "Baconora." He raised the bottle and downed a good belt of the warming stuff. He sat down on a rock and felt the cold rain seep through his ripped slicker. "I ought to ask you how it happened," he said.

The man sat up and shoved back his hat. "The road was all right when I come up to the top of the pass. It was the way down that threw me, *amigo*. The whole damned road seemed to sink under me. The sorrel dropped right from under me, I tell you. I got hold on a bush but it broke loose. I grabbed a rock but it slid with me. I was just about to let go when I saw you up there like a rescuing angel."

Burke grinned. "With a couple of days' stubble on my dirty face? Some angel!"

The man reached for the bottle and downed a drink. "The name is Jesse Lester." He grinned at Burke. "Didn't quite feel like introducing myself down there."

"Burke Dane." Burke gripped a wet hand, then corked the bottle. "We might need the rest of this later on. Looks like a long, cold night, Jesse."

"Yeh." Lester stood up. He looked down the pass. "You think we can make it?"

"I ain't about to go back."

"Yeh. You come from the east?"

"Big Bonito country."

Lester looked quickly at Burke. "You live there?"

"No, just passed through. Not much work there."

"No."

Burke untethered the dun and slung

30

the linked reatas over the pommel. "Figure I better lead him past the slide," he said.

Burke led the way, foot by foot, one hand against the rock face, listening to the irregular clattering of rock far below as the dun's hoofs displaced them. He was a good hundred yards down the road when the lightning plainly lighted it and he could see that it was solid enough, to the sight at least.

Lester came up beside him. "Not much shelter before we reach the East Fork of the Desperado," he said.

"Might as well go on then."

They were far down the pass when the odd thought came to Burke. Lester had said the road was all right when he had come to the *top* of the pass but it was the way *down* that had thrown him. He couldn't have been hanging there long, so he must have come up the pass after dusk. Why would a man ride up that exposed pass on such a night, only to turn back again rather than to descend the other side of it?

Burke glanced back at Lester. He was young, hardly more than in his early twenties, blonde and gray-eyed, and damned handsome to boot. He didn't look much like the rough and tumble type of cowpoke common to the Rio Desperado country.

There was a sagging shack not far from the bridge that spanned the rushing East Fork. While Burke took care of the dun in the lean-to, Lester went inside the shack and started a fire in the stove. Burke came in after him and shut the door. Lester had lighted the stub of a candle in the neck of a wax encrusted bottle. "Ain't much," he said cheerfully, "but we call it home, Burke."

Burke stripped off his slicker and coat. He shivered. "Poke up the fire," he said. "I see a can of Arbuckle's on the shelf. Anything in it?"

Jester grinned. "Just enough coffee for a potful."

The grateful warmth began to flow about them. Lester began to prepare the coffee. It was then that Burke noticed that the kid wore twin holsters hung from a buscadero belt. One of the holsters was empty, but the other revealed an ivory gun butt. Lester saw Burke looking at the empty sheath. "Lost it down the mountainside," he said. "Matched pair too. Cost me plenty to replace it."

"No problem for me," said Burke dryly. "I've only got one."

The kid placed the pot on the table. "Gotta get some water," he said.

"That shouldn't be any problem. Hold it under that leak in the corner." Burke grinned.

While the coffee was brewing the kid pulled off his fine boots and placed them near the stove. "You aiming to stay in this country, Burke?"

"Depends."

"What's your line?"

Burke grinned. "Well, I ain't a whiskey drummer, kid."

Jesse flushed. "Well, I meant do you do anything besides work cattle?"

"What else is there to do?"

Lester peeled off his wet socks. "You

33

look like you know how to use that sixshooter."

Burke narrowed his eyes. "What do you mean?"

"A man who can handle guns can get work a helluva lot faster in the Rio Desperado country than just a plain vaguero, *amigo*."

"I've heard that," said Burke. "I ain't a gunfighter, Jesse."

The kid's gray eyes studied Burke. "Now you ain't pulling my leg are you, Burke?"

Burke reached for his tobacco sack. "Why should I?" he said. The kid was probing too damned much. Maybe he knew something about Burke. Something he didn't let on. What the hell *had* he been doing up that pass anyway?

"I've seen your breed too many times to get fooled," said the kid.

"Maybe this time you are wrong."

The kid got two cups from a dusty shelf and wiped them out with his silk scarf. "I ain't usually wrong," he said. "You see, Burke, it's my business to know people like you."

"Meaning?"

Lester filled the two cups and placed one before Burke, then accepted one of the two quirlies Burke had fashioned. He lighted it and eyed Burke through the swirling smoke. "You don't think I poke cows for a living, do you?"

Burke grinned. "With *two* guns hanging in the way?" He glanced at the kid's clothing. "And in *that* fancy rig?"

Jesse Lester flushed a little. "I like good clothes," he said softly, "and good guns, fine horseflesh and plenty of money."

"No offense, Kid."

Lester blew out a smoke ring. "That's why I was up in the pass tonight. I suppose you were wondering about that too?"

Burke blew out a cloud of smoke to hide the expression on his face. "No," he said.

"Happens I was looking for something I lost up there."

"Such as?"

"A damned good rawhide reata. Made by Jorge Sanchez of Holbrook. Best man in the business."

Burke slowly took the cigarette from his lips. The rain was slashing down the pass and pattering steadily against the shack. The river was roaring along in flood. A gust of wind flung open the door. The kid darted to it and fought it closed.

Burke's hand dropped to his Colt. It would be so easy. He withdrew his hand before the kid turned. *Not yet* . . .

"Did you find the reata?" asked Burke quietly.

"No, dammit!"

"How'd you happen to lose it up there, of all places?"

The kid refilled his coffee cup. "One of my *amigos* borrowed it from me some time ago, then lost the damned thing. It was worth a trip up there to try and find it. Like I said; I like good things and that reata was one of them."

"You have no idea where he left it?"

asked Burke softly. His hard eyes studied the kid.

"No."

"You'd know it if you saw it?"

"I think so. Why?"

Burke shrugged. "Isn't an easy thing to identify."

"You'd know Jorge's work if you saw it."

"Yeh," said Burke. He rolled another cigarette and passed the makings to Jesse. "Who do you work for, Kid?"

"Ben Hinch." Jesse glanced quickly at Burke.

Burke lighted his cigarette. There was no expression on his face.

"You never heard of him?" asked Jesse.

"Can't say that I have, Kid."

"He's about the *biggest* man in this country, *amigo*."

"So?" Burke had always prided himself on his poker face and this time he surely needed it. Print Campbell had told him plenty about Ben Hinch, and none of it to Hinch's credit.

"I can put in a good word for you, Burke," said Jesse.

Burke drained his coffee cup. "I said I wasn't a gunfighter, Kid."

"What makes you think Ben Hinch needs gunfighters? You just said you never heard of him."

Burke looked at the kid. "You said you didn't poke cows for a living. With two guns hanging on you, I figured you were a gunfighter. So I figured Ben Hinch, whoever he is, had need of gunfighters. It's as simple as that." Burke smiled easily.

"Are you looking for work?" asked the kid flatly.

"I ain't sure. What difference does it make?"

Jesse got up and poked the fire. He dumped in more wood. "Ben Hinch usually likes to know what strangers are doing in this country," he said over his shoulder.

"I mind my own business."

The kid turned and his gray eyes were as hard as steel. "You might be able to fool some people, Burke. You aren't a saddle tramp. You aren't a common cowpoke. What are you? Gambler? Gunfighter? *Lawman?*"

Burke leaned forward. "I mind my own business, Kid," he said quietly, and his eyes were as hard as Lester's. "Maybe you ought to try it."

For a long moment the kid stood there, and then he smiled. "Forget it, *amigo*. I was only trying to pay you back for saving my life up there. Thought I'd help you along the way. You mind your own business and I'll mind mine. Keno?"

"Keno." Burke stood up. "I got a blanket roll on the dun. I'll bring it in. We might as well hole up here until dawn."

Burke closed the door behind him and hurried to the dun. He took the linked lines, hastily coiled his grass rope and fastened it to the saddle, then coiled the rawhide reata and placed it in the bottom of his saddlebag, beneath his extra gear. He took the blanket roll back into the shack. He gave Jesse one of the blankets.

The kid bedded down on the floor, letting Burke take the bunk. Burke blew out the candle and lay with his arms behind his head, staring up at the ceiling.

He wasn't so sure of himself now. Ben Hinch ran the Rio Desperado country and Jesse Lester was one of his boys. The rawhide reata was the only clue Burke had to help him find the man, or men who had lynched Charley, and he was quite sure in his mind that Jesse Lester owned that fine reata. Jesse was curious, perhaps downright suspicious of Burke, despite the fact that Burke had saved his life. Evidently the Rio Desperado country was the kind of place where a man had to take sides, because there was no neutral ground.

The wind moaned about the shack. A spit of icy rain came through a crack in the wall and touched Burke's face. The kid turned restlessly on the floor. The river roared steadily and the trees thrashed. It promised to be a wild night.

Burke closed eyes. He was dead beat;

but too full of confused thought to sleep. It was going to be a long night for him.

The kid moved. "Burke?" he said.

"Yes?"

"So long as you're a friend of Jesse Lester," he said, "you don't have to worry too much about Ben Hinch."

"Thanks, Kid."

"Forget it, *amigo*." Jesse rolled over and pulled the blanket over his head.

Burke wet his lips. As long as he was a friend of Jesse Lester's he wouldn't have to worry too much about Ben Hinch. But supposing Jesse had lied about that reata business? Supposing he had gone up there to retrieve his prized reata from the neck of a man he helped lynch?

The wind howled in diabolical glee down Windy Pass, almost as though anticipating the events that would take place when Burke Dane tried to find the murderers of his brother in the valley of the Rio Desperado.

3

"THAT'S the West Fork of the Desperado," said Jesse Lester over Burke's shoulder. "Piñon is just beyond those trees there. You can see the smoke. Maybe Piñon ain't much, but we call it home."

Burke nodded sourly. A cup of last night's rank coffee, laced with Baconora was hardly enough breakfast to hold a man on a twenty mile ride in the cold morning light. Besides, he had not slept well, and the thought of riding double a good part of that twenty miles with a man who might have put the noose about Charley's neck was hardly conducive to pleasant thought.

Piñon was pleasant enough in the watery sunlight. It spread along both sides of the road from Windy Pass, which became a little more dignified, as well as wider, to form the main street of Piñon.

The town was larger than Burke had anticipated it would be, with new, false-fronted buildings between older log structures. Somewhere beyond the town was the sawmill, with the resinous odor of freshly cut pine drifting on the morning breeze mingling with the raveled smoke.

"We'd better get some breakfast before we go to see Ben Hinch," said Jesse. He slid from behind Burke and stretched, then walked beside the tired dun to a hitching rail in front of a combination saloon and restaurant. "The Mecca," said Jesse. He grinned. "Some Mecca. But the food is good."

"I ain't fussy," said Burke. He dismounted. The dun hung his head and Burke patted it. "Thanks, *amigo*." He turned to join Jesse.

The kid was eyeing a rangy gray that was tethered farther down the rail. His eyes were half closed. He drew his Colt and twirled the cylinder to check the loads. He sheathed the fine handgun.

"What's wrong, Kid?" asked Burke quietly. "Trouble?"

43

"Nothing I can't handle."

"We can go somewhere else."

The kid turned slowly to face Burke. "I said it was nothing that I couldn't handle," he said sharply.

"I ain't hungry enough to go looking for trouble," said Burke. He knew the signs.

"It ain't your fight, *if* it comes to a fight."

Burke shrugged. He took out the makings and rolled a cigarette. "I thought this was Ben Hinch's town," he said casually.

"It is."

"You're a Hinch man, Jesse."

Jesse jerked his head toward the gray. "The man that owns that gray, is, or rather *was*, a Hinch man."

"So?"

Jesse shrugged. "I cost him his job. He won't forget it. He's been warned to stay away from Piñon. Guess he doesn't warn easy."

Burke lighted the cigarette. "Wouldn't it be just as easy to eat somewhere else?"

"You scairt?"

Burke walked up to the boardwalk and across it to the double doors of the saloon. He opened one of them and walked in. The kid grinned, then followed him.

Burke sat down at a table near the window. The bartender glanced at him. "Jenny!" he called out. Then he turned to see Jesse framed in the doorway and his fat face paled a little. He glanced quickly at a man who stood at the far end of the bar facing the doorway. The man was tall and dark. His right hand held a whiskey glass and his eyes were fixed on Jesse.

"Hello, Moss," said Jesse easily.

Moss put down the whiskey glass. He stared at Jesse.

The waitress bustled out of the kitchen towards Burke's table, then she saw Jesse. She smiled quickly, and the smile faded as she glanced back over a plump shoulder toward Moss.

"I spoke to you, Moss," said Jesse.

"I heard you," said the tall man.

Burke quietly moved his chair back. He

looked up at the waitress and jerked his head toward the kitchen. She turned slowly and walked toward the kitchen with her plump bottom waggling a little, wanting to run, but too afraid to start.

"I was looking for you last night," said Moss to Jesse.

"I wasn't here, Moss."

"Yeh. I thought for a while you just might have taken off over Windy Pass to get away from me, Lester."

"You know better than that, Moss."

"Yeh." The tall man smiled a little, but there was no mirth in his dark eyes. "I had a feeling you'd be back. Windy Pass ain't no place for a man like you if he has any conscience at all."

"Oh my God," said the bartender. His hands shook a little. "Look, fellas, I'll buy."

Jesse slowly shook his head. "Maybe *Mister* Moss needs a drink. I don't. *Mister* Moss is doing a lot of talking this morning. Maybe a drink will loosen his tongue a little more."

Burke wanted to get out there, but he

didn't want to precipitate anything by standing up. It was likely that the man named Moss didn't know that Burke was with Jesse Lester, but if he did, he'd probably think Burke was going to side Jesse if sixshooter talk started. Burke eased his hand to his Colt and traced his dry lips with the tip of his tongue. He wished to God he had taken his hunch and stayed out of the place, but it was too late now. He could almost sniff the foul, cold smell of death in the air.

The kid was walking toward the man named Moss, supreme in his youth and his strong confidence in his skill and courage. Burke moved a little. "Sit still, you!" said Moss harshly to Burke.

"Leave him out of this," said Jesse.

Moss smiled crookedly. "You Hinch boys usually got *someone* to side you. Who's this one, Lester? Maybe he's going to replace *me*, eh?"

"That wouldn't be hard," said the kid easily. "I swear to God, Jenny back there in the kitchen could replace *you*, Moss."

Burke stood up. "This isn't my fight, Moss," he said.

Again the crooked smile. "You mean you're going to let this brave little man fight *alone?*"

Jesse leaned on the bar and he was between Burke and Moss. "Get me a glass, Dan," he said to the bartender.

Dan slid a glass along the bar. Jesse smiled at Moss. "With your permission, Mister Moss," he said. He poured himself a drink. "You're not drinking with me?"

Moss reached for the bottle. In a second, swift action began, almost too quickly for the human eye to follow. Jesse threw the whiskey from his glass at Moss' face, but the tall man was fast too. He bent his head to one side and hurled the bottle with all his strength at the cocky young face in front of him. Jesse tried to bend his head to one side but his foot slipped on the sanded floor. The thick base of the bottle caught him on the left temple and he fell sideways against a table, clawing for his Colt.

Moss grinned coldly as he jumped from

behind the end of the bar and slapped leather. He crouched and aimed from the waist at the kid's bleeding head. A shot cracked flatly. Moss slowly fell forward. His gun roared from reflex action of fingers on trigger and the slug buried itself in the floor inches from Jesse's head. Moss struck the floor and lay still. Blood flowed from his body and formed a widening pool; sucked up greedily by the sand. Powdersmoke swirled in the draft and then flowed in rifted layers toward the windows.

The bartender looked with wide eyes at Burke Dane. "For the love of God," he said in a low, tense voice. "That was impossible!" He looked at the smoking Colt in Burke's hand, then up at the hard blue eyes, and he did not like what he saw. He fumbled beneath the bar and got a glass. He filled it with rye and downed it swiftly. Beads of sweat formed on his fat face.

"Pour me one, too," said Burke. He sheathed his Colt. It was then that he saw the broad-shouldered man standing framed in the doorway. Burke hesitated.

"It's all right," said Dan. "It's Matt Foxx, Ben Hinch's foreman."

Foxx nodded at Burke. "I saw what happened," he said. "I knew Moss was in here waiting for the Kid. When I saw you and the Kid come in here I came right over. Almost too late at that." Foxx eyed Burke. "If it hadn't been for you, Moss would have killed the Kid."

Foxx grinned a little. "Of course you would'a killed him right after, eh?"

Burke walked to the bar and looked down at the man he had just killed. "No," he said quietly. "It would have been too late then. I would have let the law take care of Mister Moss."

"Yeh," said Dan dryly. "The *law*."

Foxx shot a hard look at the bartender. "Send a man over to the undertaker, Dan. Get that stiff out of here."

Burke downed his drink, then refilled the glass. He knelt beside Jesse. The kid opened his eyes. "I saw Moss aiming for me, Burke," he said weakly. "Couldn't do a damned thing about it. Passed out. Thanks again, Burke."

Foxx was standing beside them. "What do you mean '*again*', Jesse?" he asked curiously.

Jesse gripped Burke by the shoulder and pulled himself up into a sitting position. "Mister Dane has a habit of saving my life, Matt. Second time in twenty four hours."

Burke stood up. "You couldn't help the first time, Jesse," he said quietly. "You walked into this one. Damned fool stunt if I ever saw one."

Jesse's eyes narrowed. "There was no way out of it, Burke," he said.

"You could have stayed out of here."

The kid got shakily to his feet and touched the swelling on his forehead. "You don't know me very well."

"Amen," said Matt.

"You'd better not move the body until the sheriff gets here," said Burke. A pounding, stabbing headache suddenly began to lance through his skull. It had been a long hard trail, and an uncomfortable night, climaxed with a killing; a killing by Burke Dane, who had been soul weary of killing, for this was not the first man he had killed, nor, he thought, would it be the last if he kept following the devious and bloody trail he had embarked upon.

"It's all right," said Matt. "It was self-defense, wasn't it?"

"Not for me," said Burke. He looked at the stocky foreman. "It wasn't my fight."

"Justifiable homicide then," said Foxx.

"You talk like a lawyer," said Burke. "I still think you ought to get the sheriff."

The kid grinned. "Matt is the deputy-sheriff in these parts," he said.

"I thought he was foreman for Ben Hinch," said Burke.

"He does that too," said Dan the bartender.

Burke wet his lips and reached for the rye bottle. "Very convenient," he said.

"What do you mean by that?" asked Matt Foxx after apause.

Burke looked up into the man's hard green eyes. A tension had suddenly come into the drafty barroom.

"Well, mister?" demanded Foxx.

Burke looked away. "Nothing, mister. Nothing at all." But he knew well enough he hadn't put Matt Foxx off the track. It had been a damn fool thing for Burke to say, but then he had a reputation for doing just such things. He'd have to watch that tendency in the Valley of the Rio Desperado.

"Let's eat," said the kid suddenly.

Burke turned slowly. "With *that* on the floor?" he asked.

Jesse grinned. "You act like you never seen a dead man before."

"I've seen a few here and there," said Burke.

"Jenny!" called out Jesse. "Ham and eggs for two! Get us started with a pot of jamoke!"

Matt Foxx poured himself a drink.

"Don't forget Moss had a couple of good *compañeros*, Kid," he said.

"No."

"They haven't done anything that would make Ben Hinch fire them like he fired Moss," said the foreman.

"Keno," said Jesse easily.

The green eyes probed at Jesse, "Just keep it in mind, Kid."

"I will."

The foreman left and Jesse walked to a table and sat down.

Burke rolled a smoke and sat down across from the Kid. He handed him the makings and watched the Kid deftly roll a quirly. "What did he mean, Jesse?" asked Burke.

"Curly Carter and Larry Newman. They were *amigos* with Joe Moss there. Fact is, Larry was his cousin."

"Great, oh great," said Burke.

"They don't like me either," said the Kid.

"I wonder why?" asked Burke softly. "Why did Joe Moss lose his job with Hinch?"

"He got fresh with my sister, Burke."

"So he loses a job and then he gets killed."

The Kid quickly pulled the draw string of the tobacco bag with his even white teeth but his gray eyes were fixed on Burke. "I'll kill any man who gets fresh with Belle," he said quietly. He lighted his cigarette. "Anyone. *Comprende?*"

Burke shrugged and then nodded. "I wasn't figuring on getting fresh with any woman," he said.

Jenny bustled in and placed the coffee pot on the table. She filled two cups. Her wide hip brushed against Jesse. His hand moved swiftly. She jerked a little and her face reddened "Now, Mister Lester," she said chidingly, but it didn't seem as though her heart was in it. Then she jerked again. "*Mister* Lester! You ain't no gentleman!"

The Kid grinned "Can't help it Jenny. When I see a target I just got to try a shot at it."

"Mister Lester!" She marched off, her hips waggling defiantly.

"Ain't you the one," said Burke dryly. "A few minutes ago a man died because he got fresh with *your* sister."

Jesse sipped at his coffee. "Jenny likes it," he said.

"Your sister must be pretty lonely"

"Why do you say that?"

"Hellsfire, a man would be loco to chase after her with you hanging around in the background breathing fire and smoke."

"Wait'll you see Belle," said the Kid. "Just wait."

The stiffening body was removed before the two of them were served, for which Burke was duly grateful. It didn't seem to matter one way or another to the Kid.

"Let's go home and clean up," said the Kid. He paid for the meal and winked at Jenny. She giggled, but kept her tempting hips away from his quick hands.

Burke untethered the dun and led him along the street. Here and there men watched them and Burke sensed a definite feeling of hostility emanating from some of them. It didn't seem to bother Jesse Lester though. He walked easily, with a cigarette dangling from the corner of his mouth, trading look for look with every man, and it was the others who looked away first. Then Burke remembered some of the information told to him by blind Print Campbell. Ben Hinch ran that country like a feudal lord, but there were men who hated his guts because of it. Trouble was, Ben had the money, the power, and the fighting guns to back him up.

Jesse turned down a side street and stopped in front of a pretty little frame cottage, fenced in with pickets and with window boxes in the windows. "Home," he said. He glanced at Burke. "This is your home as long as you stick around, Burke."

"I wasn't figuring on leaving right away," said Burke, "but I don't aim to wear out my welcome."

Burke tethered the dun to the fence and followed the Kid up the walk to the porch. He opened the door. "Belle!" he called out. "I'm home! Got company!"

Burke walked into the neat little living room and looked about. If Belle Lester kept a place like this she'd make a good wife for some staid businessman, or maybe a sky pilot. Then he saw her, framed in the doorway to the kitchen, and he knew right then and there that the Kid had not been joshing when he had said, "Wait'll you see Belle. Just wait."

There wasn't any doubt that she was Jesse Lester's sister. Her coloring was the same, and she had the same fine blonde hair and clear gray eyes. She looked enough like Jesse to be his twin, except she must be some years older, but still a young woman. She wore a split riding skirt, white shirt open at the throat, a short leather jacket, and small figured boots. A hat hung at her back, from a leather strap about her shapely neck. She was a beauty. Burke wasn't quite sure he had ever seen one quite like her. He had seen lovelier women of course, but the combination of her coloring, her features and configuration was enough to make any man stop and look at her.

"You can close your mouth now, Burke," said Jesse with a sly grin. "This is my sister Belle. Belle, this is Mister Burke Dane."

Burke was acutely conscious of his unshaven face and general trail dirtiness as he took off his Stetson and bowed his head. "Mighty pleased, Miss Lester," he said.

There was a slight iciness in her expression as she nodded her lovely head. "Mister Dane," she said in a voice that seemed to have the ringing quality of a silver bell. She looked at Jesse. "I was just about to leave for Windy Pass, Jesse. Why didn't you come back last night?"

"Seems as though I ran out of road, sis."

"What do you mean?"

Jesse quickly explained what had happened. There was a softer look about Belle now. She thanked Burke warmly. "Jesse insisted on going up there yesterday after that silly rope of his. I can't understand why he couldn't get another one."

Evidence, thought Burke. Evidence that he had hung one man and might yet put a rope about Jesse Lester's own neck.

She looked at her brother. "Joe Moss came back to Piñon last night," she said quietly. "I wanted to warn you about him, Jesse."

"You're a little late," he said.

She eyed him closely. "What do you mean, Jesse?"

"We already ran into him."

Her lovely eyes flickered toward the swelling on his forehead. "He was saying that he'd kill you on sight, Jesse."

"He meant to," said the Kid.

She glanced at Burke and then back at her brother. "Where is he now, Jesse?" she demanded.

Jesse dropped into a chair and thrust his slim legs out in front of him. "Mister Farrier, our esteemed mortician, has him in charge, sis."

She paled a little. "You *killed* him, Jesse?"

"Not *me*. My partner Burke did the job. Saved my life twice in twenty-four hours."

Burke flushed. "He would have killed your brother in cold blood, ma'am," he said. The look on her face repelled him, but he was game. "Don't you see? I had to kill him."

"I see all right," she said quietly. "I see killing all the time in this country. Where will it end? Those who live by the sword . . ."

"Your brother is safe," said Burke dryly. "It was him or Joe Moss."

She glanced down at the tied-down sixgun and at the brown capable hand of Burke Dane, then looked up into his bitter blue eyes. "Who are you?" she asked suddenly. "Why have you come here? What have you to do with my brother?"

Burke had the eerie feeling that she was seeing right through him, as though she knew something; *something that Jesse Lester did not know.* He picked up his hat. "I'll be seeing you, Jesse," he said. "Happy to have met you, ma'am."

"You're staying here with us until I get you a job with Ben Hinch," said Jesse quickly.

"No," said Burke. "I'll find my own place here in Piñon."

"You might find a place to stay, you won't get nothing but a two-bit job unless you work for Ben Hinch."

"I'll chance it," said Burke.

"You're driving him away, Belle!" said Jesse angrily.

She came closer to Burke. "Thanks for saving my brother's life," she said. "Please stay."

He walked to the door and opened it. "I'm sorry," he said. "See you later, Jesse." He closed the door behind him and walked to the gate. He stepped over it and mounted the dun after untethering it. He kneed the big horse out into the middle of the street and rode back toward the main street of Piñon.

Belle Lester came out onto the porch

and looked after Burke. "Who is that man, Jesse?" she said.

"I told you. Burke Dane."

"Where did he come from?"

"*Quien sabe?* From New Mexico Territory is all I know." He eyed her. "Why do you ask?"

She tapped her quirt against the side of her leg. "I don't really know. He isn't any run of the mill saddle tramp. There is something secret about that man."

"Oh, cut it out, sis! Burke is all right. I'll get him a job with Ben Hinch. After what Burke did this morning, Ben won't hesitate to hire Burke. He's fast, Belle! I didn't see him, but Joe Moss had his sixgun out and cocked when Burke fired. Dropped him like nothing."

She walked toward the stable at the rear of the lot. "Faster than *you*, Jesse?" she asked over her shoulder.

He stared at her. "What do you mean?"

She turned. "No one in this valley seems to be quite as fast as you, Jesse. Ben Hinch says that. Everyone said that except Joe Moss. Joe Moss was fast, wasn't he, Jesse?"

"Yes. '

"As fast as you? '

"Pretty close, Belle," admitted the Kid.

"And this man, this Burke Dane, from nowhere, drew and killed him when Joe had his gun out and cocked?"

Jesse half closed his eyes. "Yeh," he said softly. "Yeh. He said he wasn't a gunfighter."

She had saddled her mare and she mounted it and rode it up beside the porch. "I'll see Ben this morning," she said. "I'm going riding with Clete."

He flushed. "Clete Hinch? Him? He ain't no good, Belle! Ain't there any other men around Piñon you can ride with instead of him?"

She drew on a pair of gloves. "Certainly," she said, "but let's face it, Jesse. We haven't got a dime. The big money in the Rio Desperado country is in the Hinch family, and Ben Hinch won't live forever. Clete is his only man child and his pride and joy as well. I'm like you, Jesse I like nice things. I'm not a fast gun, nor a mankiller like you, but I've got some stock-in-trade." She looked down at her lovely body. "Something Clete Hinch is mighty interested in."

He smashed a fist against the side of the house. "Don't talk like that!" he rasped out.

She smiled, "I'm free, white and over twenty-one. You do your type of mankilling and I'll do mine, Jesse." She touched the mare with her heels and set it at the fence, rising gracefully over it. She galloped the mare down the center of the street, a picture of loveliness and grace, enough to turn any man's head. She turned. "It'll take a wedding ring to close the deal, dear brother," she called back, "so don't worry about your sister's virtue!"

There was a sick look on Jesse Lester's face as he watched her turn onto the main street and disappear from sight. He walked into the house and took a full bottle from a cabinet. The bottle was half empty before he fell asleep in the big platform rocker.

Another man had watched Belle Lester ride past. Burke Dane had seen her through the dusty window of a corner saloon. He had the uneasy feeling that Belle Lester had seen through him as he had seen through the streaked window glass. He looked down at his drink and seemed to see her lovely oval face framed in the amber fluid. He downed the drink and placed a coin beside the empty glass. The whiskey seemed to sicken him. "Where can I get a room?" he asked the barkeep.

"Upstairs. Piñon House. Ain't much, but it's better than sleeping in a barn. Not much better though, Mister." The man grinned. "Then there's the Hinch Hotel."

"Owned by Ben Hinch?"

"Yeh." The man grinned again. "Happens he owns the Piñon House too."

"And this saloon?"

"I rent the place, Mister. He owns the building."

Burke nodded. "Mister Hinch seems to be the big frog in the puddle around here."

The flat eyes of the bartender studied him. "After what you done this morning, maybe Ben Hinch will own you too, Mister."

Burke shrugged. He walked to the door.

"If he makes you an offer, take it, Mister," called the bartender.

"And if I *don't?*"

The man picked up the glass, rinsed it and wiped it. He set it neatly atop a group of other glasses. "Then get on your hoss, aim it east, west, north or south and keep agoin'."

The man's words stuck in Burke's mind as he left the bar and led the tired dun to the livery stable. He signed in at the Piñon House, getting a corner room with a view up and down the main street as well as the street upon which Jesse and Belle Lester lived.

There was one other thing he did before he bathed and shaved; he checked the back entrance to the hotel. A man never knew when he might have sudden and important need of such knowledge.

4

IT was dusk when Burke awoke to hear the faint pattering of rain upon the windows. He sat up and shivered in the damp cold. He dressed in fresh clothing and walked to the front window to look down upon the main street. Yellow lamplight shone through the misty rain slanting down upon the town. Lightning flickered against the dark and lowering skies. Burke rolled a cigarette and was just about to light it when he saw the man standing in a doorway across the street—the sixth sense born in a man who lives a hard and dangerous life immediately alerted Burke. He took the cigarette from his lips. He walked to the door and placed an ear against it. There was no sound from the hallway.

He swung his gunbelt about his lean waist, buckled it, then checked his Colt. He put on his coat and slicker, placing a double-barreled derringer in his left coat pocket for extra insurance. Burke left the hotel by the back entrance, coming quietly down the long stairway to the muddy alleyway. He squelched through the mud to the eastern end of the alley, cut up the intersection, crossed the main street swiftly and then walked west along the alleyway behind the buildings on the side of the street opposite his hotel until he reached the next intersection. He walked to the corner and looked at the man in the doorway. The man was too busy watching Burke's hotel window to see the tall, hard-faced man watching him. Burke stepped into a nearby doorway as another man left the saloon across the street and came across to the watcher.

Burke pulled down his hat brim and turned up his slicker collar. The wind was blowing toward him from the two men.

"You see him yet, Harv?" asked the man from the saloon.

"Hell no! He's either dead asleep or dead drunk, Curly."

Curly spat into the gutter. "Jesus, I ain't got a mind to stay here all night waitin' for him to leave that room."

"What's your beef? You been sitting in Garvey's saloon whilst I been standing out here in the wet?"

"Yeh, well maybe you'd like to try the saloon awhile?"

Harv shook his head. "From what I heard about this *hombre*, I don't want no likker in me if he comes agunnin', Curly."

"Maybe he was just lucky," suggested Curly.

Harv shook his head again. "That's not what Dan Phipps said. Godfrey! Joe Moss had the Kid down on the sawdust, as whoozy as a drunk, and Joe had his cutter in his hand, cocked too, when this *hombre* draws and shoots! Joe would'a killed the Kid if it hadn't been for this Dane *hombre*."

Curly rolled a cigarette while he looked up at the window of Dane's room. "Yeh. But it was what he said to Matt Foxx that puzzles me. That was after Matt ast' him

71

if he would'a killed Joe after Joe had killed the Kid. Dane says no, that it would'a been too late then, that he would'a let the law take care of Joe. That proves he ain't no real sidekick of the Kid."

"Who *is?*" asked Harv dryly. "That conceited, swell-headed yearlin' don't want no one siding him. He's too fast! He's too good! He's tough as a boot! Yaaah!"

Curly looked nervously up and down the street. "Well, *I* ain't ascairt of him."

Harv grunted. "Not as long as Larry Newman is between you and the Kid, you ain't!"

Curly eyed the window again. He lighted his cigarette. "Let's give him another twenty minutes, then take a look up there. What the hell does Matt Foxx think we'll find up there. From what I heard, this Dane looks almost like a saddle tramp."

"*Quien sabe?* We got our orders. You want to quit? Then you quit, and you tell Matt. I ain't going to do it!"

72

Burke faded around the corner, returning the way he had come. He entered the livery stable by the back door. The place was deserted except for a half a dozen horses. He patted the dun, then removed Jesse Lester's rope from the saddlebag. He placed the rope beneath his slicker and left the stable the same way he had entered it, to return to his room. He stripped off coat and slicker, then lighted the Argand lamp. Burke rolled a cigarette and puttered about the room, taking as much time as a man would normally take to get dressed. He knew well enough those two men were still watching the window. The rain slashed against the side of the frame building as he put out the lamp and walked into the hall. He knew full well they would examine his belongings once he left the room, but there was nothing there to cast suspicion on him. Nothing more than his dirty trail clothing, personals and other odds and ends any man would carry with him while traveling. The only incriminating thing on him, in the eyes of *those* men, in any case, would be the fine rope he had found about his brother's neck in Windy Pass. It was quite likely they'd also check his horse gear. The cold thought struck him that they might already have done so. He'd risk it; he'd *have* to risk it.

Thinking of the rope gave him an idea. He walked to the rear entrance and out onto the back porch. A clothes line was strung from post to post. He cut the wet and stiff knots and tied the line across the top of the flight of stairs, about six inches high. "Diabolical," he said with a crooked grin.

Burke re-entered the deserted hotel. The place was as quiet as a cliff-dwelling ruin, and there was no sign of the clerk in his cubbyhole at the bottom of the front stairs. Burke stepped out into the street and lighted another cigarette, spotting Harv and Curly in their doorway across the drizzling street. Burke walked leisurely down the street, like a man looking for a good eating place. He entered a restaurant at the corner, bought a couple of sacks of makings, then left by the side entrance. He walked back to the corner just in time to see Harv and Curly enter the Piñon House.

Burke walked slowly toward the hotel, giving the boys time to get to work. He walked into the entrance and saw the clerk. There was a startled look on the man's face, and Burke knew then and there the man was a willing party to the surreptitious search going on upstairs. "You're back quickly," he said nervously.

"Forgot my wallet," said Burke. "Can't get grub without dinero."

"No need for you to go upstairs," said the clerk hastily. "I can grubstake you, Mister Dane."

"That's right nice of you."

"It's all right."

Burke glanced up the stairs. "On second thought I might want to try the games tonight. I'll need a little gambling money." He started up the stairs.

"Wait!" called out the man. He came around the desk. "How much will you need?"

"A hundred anyway."

"I haven't got that much here but I can get it in the saloon."

Burke turned slowly. "By that time I could have my wallet," he said with a smile.

The man could not meet his gaze. "All right, Mister Dane," he said in a loud, carrying voice. "You have your room key?"

"Yes," said Burke. He trod heavily on the stairs.

He heard the room door swing open and the quick thudding of booted feet on the thinly carpeted flooring of the hall. Just as his head reached the floor level he saw the two shadowy figures at the end of the hall. They tore open the door. There was a loud yell from the first man, followed by an explosive curse from the second man. Something thudded and crashed down the outside stairway and a man screamed harshly.

Burke casually walked into his room and looked about by the light of a match. The dresser drawers gaped open. The mattress was off center. The room stank of candle grease. Burke closed the door behind him and walked down the stairs. "Sounds like a fight in the alleyway," he said pleasantly to the white-faced clerk who was coming up the stairs, two at a time. "None of my business. Take my advice and stay out of it."

He grinned as he closed the outer door behind him. Burke took plenty of time to eat and enjoy his dinner. He bought a couple of good cigars, thrust one between his even white teeth and lighted it, then strolled leisurely back toward Garvey's saloon. The rain had stopped and a cold wind swept along the muddy street. He entered the saloon. A drunk sat at a rear table with his head resting on his folded arms. Another man sat in a chair tilted back against the rear wall reading a newspaper. There were two more customers in the place and there was no doubt who they were. Harv and Curly stood at the end of the bar. Curly had a wet cloth at the back of his neck and had his head held back. Blood stained his face and scarf. There was a large swelling on his forehead and his lip was split. Harv was nursing his left arm and his face was swollen on the left side.

"Beer," said Burke easily to the bartender. It was the same man who had served him that morning.

"Comin' up. You get your room all right?"

Burke nodded. He jerked a thumb upward. "Right overhead, on the corner. A little drafty but it has a nice view." He managed to keep a straight face as two pairs of eyes shot suspicious glances at him.

"Like I said," remarked the bartender. "It ain't much, but it's better than sleeping in a barn. You find a job yet?"

"How'd you know I was looking for one?"

The bartender shrugged. "Figured you was. You remember what I told you about any offers?"

"You mean Mister Hinch is looking for help?"

Again the two pairs of eyes flicked at him.

"He usually is." Garvey glanced at Harv and Curly. "That right, boys?"

Curly grunted. Harv shrugged. "You'd have to ask Mister Hinch."

Garvey grinned. "Oh, he'll give this fella a job all right." He looked at Curly. "How's your nose?"

"How's yours?" growled Curly.

"The boys fell over some stuff in the alley," said Garvey in a low voice. "At least that's what *they* say." He wiped the bar. "Jesse Lester was in here awhile back, looking for you, Mister Dane. I told him I thought you had a room upstairs. He said he'd meet you down at the bar and grille in the Hinch Hotel."

"Sounds very elegant," said Burke dryly. He downed his beer and walked toward the door just in time to see a tall, lean man walk in, dart a look toward the two sorry looking characters at the far end of the bar, then fix Burke with a hard set look. Burke instantly knew this type. It was the same breed as Joe Moss and in fact the man resembled Joe Moss a little.

"Have a drink, Larry," said Harv.

A cold feeling came over Burke. *Larry*. It must be Larry Newman, Joe Moss' cousin. The hard flat eyes held Burke's almost as though trying to force him to look away. Then Newman stepped aside. "Matt Foxx wants to see you boys," he said to the pair at the end of the bar.

Burke had his hand on the door knob when Newman spoke again. "Wait, you," he said in a low voice.

Burke turned slowly. "Yes?"

"You're Dane, aren't you?"

"Yes."

Newman looked up and down Burke, "A fast gun, eh?"

"Fast enough," said Burke easily. "I'm not anxious to try and prove it."

"Like you did this morning, eh?"

Burke shook his head wearily. "Moss was going to kill the Kid."

"And you killed Moss. *Just like that*, eh?"

"I don't want no trouble in here," said Garvey.

"Shut up!" snapped Newman. He studied Burke. "There won't be no trouble. *Now*, anyway. I don't know who or what you are, Mister Dane, but Joe Moss was my cousin. The Kid had a gun whipping coming to him. He'll get it yet. He was lucky this morning."

"You seem to forget that it was more than a whipping he was going to get, Newman," said Burke quietly. "Moss was going to kill him, not pistol-whip him."

"Was it any business of yours?"

"I don't like murder."

"Then you come to the wrong place, by Godfrey," said Harv.

"Who are you trying to fool, Dane?" asked Newman. "I know your type. You aren't any saddle tramp looking for twenty-five a month and found. Who are you?"

Burke smiled gently. "How long have you been appointed official nose around here, Newman?"

"Oh my God," said Garvey.

Larry Newman smiled thinly. "I'll remember that too, Dane. Right now I've got things to do. But I won't forget you, Dane. Ever . . ."

Burke walked outside and relighted his cigar. Like a damned fool he had jumped into this mess with both feet, and with closed eyes. It would have been easier to drift into town and get any kind of job until he was ready to make his move, but rescuing Jesse Lester in Windy Pass, then saving him from being killed by Joe Moss had put him right in the local limelight, and there wasn't a thing he could do about it. There was no use in backtrailing unless he wanted to forget his mission to get Charley's money and find his killers. That he could not do.

There was one thing he knew for certain. A man was either with Ben Hinch and his *corrida* or he was against them. There was no neutral ground in the Rio Desperado country. Print Campbell had assured him of that in no uncertain terms. Burke wasn't so sure he wanted to ally himself with such men as Jesse Lester,

Harv and Curly, and the man he had just faced in Garvey's saloon; the man named Larry Newman. Newman was stiff-legged with the hackles up and it wouldn't take much to trip the hair trigger of his intent to pay off the blood score for the death of his cousin, Joe Moss.

The night life of Piñon was flickering up as Burke walked slowly toward the imposing pile of the Hinch Hotel. One could hardly miss it. The streets were empty of local ranchers and townspeople. The shops were closed but the saloons and gambling halls were flooded with light, thick with tobacco smoke and bursting with the mingled cacophony of player pianos, clinking glassware, rattling poker chips, tumbling chuck-a-luck cages and whirring roulette wheels. Patient, hipshot horses stood in rows at the hitching racks; their wet hides glistening in the lamplight.

Burke peeled off his worn slicker in a doorway, wrapped it about Lester's rawhide rope, and stuffed slicker and rope into a hollow area in the ramada shelter above his head in front of a leather goods shop. He walked along the boardwalk to the hotel and saw the side entrance that opened into the bar and grille. He glanced into the big lobby of the hotel. It was well carpeted, filled with overstuffed furniture, lighted by crystal chandeliers and fine table lamps on marble-topped tables. Very elegant.

Burke flipped his cigar butt into the gutter, straightened his string tie and walked into the bar and grille. Ben Hinch had done himself proud in this establishment as well as the rest of the Hinch Hotel. For the moment Burke almost thought he was in one of the plushier joints of Albuquerque, El Paso, or Fort Worth. The two bartenders were replete in white mess jackets, waxed mustaches and varnished hair. The bar itself was a mahogany masterpiece, backed by a full length mirror set with an array of glittering glassware and polished silver utensils. Well, pardon me all to hell, thought Dane as he saw the thick carpeting on the floor and the massive garboons softly reflecting the glow of the many lamps. The light also caressed the naked shoulders of half a dozen women in various booths, and Burke wasn't sure whether they were guests or high class *filles* working for the house.

Burke hung his hat on a brass hook and walked toward the rear of the establishment followed by the half bold, half coy looks of the women, and the curious, half challenging looks of some of the men. He heard the soft laughter of Jesse Lester and saw him sitting in a booth with a woman who was dressed to the nines in red, and with her dark glossy hair piled up, highlights showing as she moved her head. The Kid grinned as he saw Burke. "You're getting 'way behind, *compañero*," he said. His eyes flashed. He had been playing the bottle that evening. He placed a hand on the naked shoulder of the girl, for she was hardly more than that, and looked up at Burke. "Sally, this is Burke Dane, my good friend. Burke, this is Sally Depree, belle of Hinch's Hotel."

Young as the girl was, and lovely in the soft glow of the lamps, there was a hardness in her wide green eyes. "Jesse has been telling me about you," she said, a little breathlessly. She held out a slim hand and as Burke took it he felt the slight pressure that conveyed everything, or *almost* everything he had to know about her. As she moved to look at Jesse the locket she wore about her lovely neck swung and rested in the deep cleft of her high young breasts and Burke Dane's eyes became riveted on it.

"Sit down, Burke," said Jesse. "We're drinking sangarees. What about you?"

Burke nodded. "I'll have the same." He sat down opposite the girl. She flicked those lovely green eyes at him. Burke had been around. He had seen the elephant in many a dive and joint from Fort Worth to Yuma, but he had never seen a lovelier specimen of her shameless breed than this girl.

"Burke Dane," she said musingly. "I'm almost tempted to ask if that is your *real* name, Mister Dane."

"It is as far as we're concerned, Sal," said Jesse.

"Why did you say that?" asked Burke of the girl.

She narrowed her eyes a little. "It sound almost familiar."

"Jesse has been telling you about me, you said. Maybe too much, Miss Sally. Memory plays strange tricks."

"I suppose you are right." She placed her lovely mouth at the rim of her glass and sipped her sangaree.

But Burke Dane knew that he had not put her off. The cold feeling fled through his mind that she might know him from elsewhere, or have heard of him from some of the other girls. Members of her profession traveled widely and knew everyone. He glanced down at the locket, and she smiled, thinking he was studying the fascinating cleft just under the locket. Jesse stood up. "Excuse me," he said a little thickly. He walked toward the rear of the big room.

"You like the locket?" she asked of Dane.

"Yes." It was heart-shaped and set with small diamonds.

"Jesse gave it to me," she said carelessly. "Jesse is always trying to put his brand on me."

"He seems to be doing pretty well."

She leaned toward him and the locket swung forward, tinkling against a water carafe on the table. "I don't belong to anyone," she said softly. "Not *yet* anyway, Mister Dane."

He reached for the locket and pressed the catch. It opened before she could straighten up. Burke found himself looking at the tiny pictures of Dolly Mayo and little Alan Mayo, his niece and nephew. Sally pulled the locket from his fingers. She snapped it shut.

"Relatives?" murmured Burke quietly.

She bit a full lower lip. "I didn't even know there were any pictures in it. I thought it was new!"

Burke leaned back as the waiter placed fresh drinks on the table. He studied the girl. Maybe she *didn't* know where that locket came from. The last thing Marion

Mayo had told Burke the night before he had left the valley of the Big Bonito, was that Charley had taken the locket—a wedding gift to Marion from Burke himself—to the Rio Desperado country so that he would have the pictures of the children with him. Now here it was, about the neck of a lovely young honky-tonk girl in Piñon, given to her by Jesse Lester. There was only one way he could have gotten it.

He looked up to see the Kid weaving through the narrow aisles between the tables, waving casually to those he knew and trading bold stares with those who knew him for what he was—a hired killer with a baby face. Jesse sat down. "Ben Hinch wants to see you, Burke," he said.

Burke grinned. "You talk to him in the men's room?"

"Haw! No, he's in his office, just off the bar back there, between this room and the lobby. Better hurry."

Burke drained his glass, smiled at Sally, though there was cold murder in his heart, then walked easily back through the room toward the wide door of the office. Curious looks were directed toward him. It didn't take long in a town that size to know who a stranger was and Burke had made himself known the *big* way by killing Joe Moss that very morning.

He tapped on the door and heard a man call out, inviting him in. He opened the door and walked into a big office, paneled in fine wood, carpeted, and lighted with fine lamps. A man sat behind a paper-littered desk eyeing him. "You're Burke Dane?" he said.

"Yes,"

The man stood up and held out a hand. "Ben Hinch. Sit down. Cigar?"

Burke accepted a cigar, cut off the end of it in a silver clipper on the desk, lighted it and sat down in a deep leather chair, blowing out a ring of smoke as he did so. Ben Hinch was a medium sized man in his fifties, dark of hair and eye, cleanshaven, and successful looking. Hinch waved a hand at a small table covered with bottles. "Drink?" he said.

"Later, Mister Hinch."

Hinch nodded. "Business first, eh?"

"You're doing the talking, Mister Hinch."

"So I am. I usually do around here."

"So I've heard."

An odd, pleased sort of a look fled across the smooth face. "Jesse Lester has been telling me about you. *And* Matt Foxx, as a matter of fact. Seems as though you saved Jesse's life twice in twenty-four hours."

"Luck," said Burke quietly.

"Maybe. I can use you, Mister Dane."

"In what way, Mister Hinch? You know nothing of my capabilities."

The man leaned back in his chair and smiled coldly. "I can always use a fast gun, Mister Dane."

"That isn't my business."

Again the cold smile. "Listen, Mister Dane, I was born and raised here in the Southwest. I know men. The average cowpoke is an average shot, and far from being fast on the draw. He hasn't got the time nor the money to practice shooting to develop the deadly skill men such as yourself and Jesse Lester have developed. Now, a man with that skill, is most likely a gambler, a lawman, perhaps an outlaw, or a hired gun. Which category do *you* fall into, Mister Dane?"

"I have been a gambler, but I know many gamblers who are not fast guns, Mister Hinch."

"And the other categories?"

Burke smiled. "You leave little room for maneuvering, Mister Hinch."

"So?"

"I'm not a lawman, an outlaw, *or* a hired gun."

"You will be a hired gun if you stay in the Rio Desperado country, Mister Dane." Hinch relighted his cigar. His dark eyes probed into Burke's eyes. "Either that, or get out of this area within twenty-four hours."

"And if I don't?"

"I can't afford to have a free lance fast gun hanging around my country, Mister Dane. Like all successful men, I have made some enemies on my way to the top of the heap. Some of those enemies might just hire a man like you to fight against Ben Hinch. I can't allow that."

Burke inspected the end of his cigar. "I was under the impression I was in the Land of the Free. America, isn't it? Or did I somehow leave the States on the way here?"

Hinch leaned back in his chair. "I like a man with a sense of humor. Like the man who strung a rope across the top of the back stairs of the Piñon House earlier this evening. Rather a rough sense of humor, but justifiable under the circumstances. I might have done the same thing myself, Mister Dane."

Burke's poker face was a tribute to his years of training in the gambling halls of the Southwest.

"Well, is it a deal, Mister Burke Dane?"

Burke looked steadily at Hinch. There was no other way out.

"One hundred and fifty a month. Horses and cartridges at my expense. Frequent bonuses for jobs well done."

"Bounties?" asked Burke.

"Bonuses, Mister Dane. Is it a deal?"

Burke nodded. He gripped Hinch's extended hand. The big man smiled. "One other thing: You never *quit* a job with Ben Hinch. You get *fired*, but you never *quit*."

Burke stood up. "Very clear," he said.

Hinch waved a hand. "Report to Matt Foxx out at the ranch no later than noon tomorrow. Tonight your drinks are on the house, compliments of Ben Hinch. But be sober when you show up for work tomorrow."

"*Gracias*, Mister Hinch."

Burke walked to the door. He glanced back. Ben Hinch was already working at his papers. It had been a routine job of work for the big man. Hire a fast gun, a professional killer, put the Hinch brand on him so that nobody else in the Rio Desperado country could use him, then forget he exists until he is needed. It was as simple and mercenary as that.

5

THE rain was slanting down in a fine silky looking mist as Burke Dane stood in the deep doorway of the Hinch Hotel Bar with a cigarette dangling from the corner of his mouth. The town was quiet, almost too quiet to suit Burke Dane, even if it was three o'clock of a dark and rainy morning. Jesse Lester came out behind Burke and as he did so the door closed and the key turned in the lock.

"The last dog hung?" asked Burke sourly.

The Kid was just a little drunk, which was a surprise to Burke, for Jesse had been playing the bottle a good part of the night. The only reason Burke had stayed around was to make sure Jesse got home safely. No one but Burke Dane was going to collect the blood debt from the kid.

Jesse hunched up his slicker up about his neck. "Where's yours?" he asked.

"Forgot it," said Burke. "We can stay under the ramadas a good part of the way."

Jesse shrugged. They walked around the corner of the hotel and looked down the deserted main street. A lone pony stood hipshot at a rack. Burke and Jesse passed beneath the ramada where Burke had hastily hidden the rawhide reata. Burke's eyes flicked up and down the street. No one was in sight. They crossed the intersection and passed along the second block, across the street from Burke's hotel, and still there was no sign of life except a dog rooting in a trash pile.

They crossed the intersection at a diagonal. Burke turned and looked back toward Garvey's saloon. The place was in utter darkness. The Kid kept on and had reached the alleyway and was looking for a place to cross the muddy ruts that were running with rain water. Burke's head was beginning to clear from the tobacco smoke of the bar, and the little drinking he had done that evening, while he passed the time in a game of draw for low stakes.

Jesse jumped the ruts and cursed as he went in over his boot tops. Beyond him was the dark shell of a burned out building. Something moved within a paneless window. Something glistened in the darkness. *Shotgun*, thought Burke. He darted forward and hit the Kid with a shoulder driving him down in the mud, while he himself dropped to his knees and swept up his Colt in an easy and fluid motion. The scattergun roared, both barrels belching smoke flame and leaden death. Something invisible to Burke whipped his Stetson from his head even as he fired twice into the darkness. A man screamed harshly and it seemed to Burke he had heard someone scream like that not too long ago.

"Look out, Burke!" yelled the Kid. "Drop!"

Burke dropped into the cold and clammy mud as Jesse fired over his head. A man staggered across the street and even as he did so he fired his sixgun. The slug rapped into the burned out building. Jesse fired three more times and each of the softnosed slugs slapped into the doomed man. He pitched face forward into the mud and lay still, smoke arising from the hot muzzle of his gun.

Burke jumped to his feet and whirled as he heard boots thudding in the mud. A man jumped into a doorway just as Burke fired twice, throwing screaming lead inches behind the man. Red flame spouted in the wet darkness but the man was shooting wild. Jesse darted out into the street and slammed two shots into the doorway, but by that time the man had gotten into the building. "Stay back!" warned Burke. He walked slowly forward, pistol at hip level, searching the darkness with slitted eyes.

Jesse was swiftly reloading. He ran up beside Burke and passed him to reach the main street, then whirled and fired three times down the street. A man yelled hoarsely, then hoofs thudded in the mud of the street and faded away into the night.

Jesse turned and grinned. "Neat," he said. "Too damned bad we didn't get him too. I think I winged him though, Burke."

Burke turned and ran back toward the man lying in the street. A lamp went on in a house and a door slammed on the main street. A man shouted. Burke rolled the man over and looked into the set white face of Harv. Jesse clambered into the building. "It's Curly Carter," he said. "Dead as last night's bottle." He came back. "Let's get out of here," he added.

"Why?"

The Kid spat. "I ain't in any mood to go to a coroner's inquest on this. It was self-defense, wasn't it?"

Burke stared at the Kid. He had made sense, and Burke was already hock deep in trouble his first day in Piñon. The Kid ran up the alleyway with Burke close at his heels, like two kids fleeing the scene of a Halloween prank. Jesse darted up a passageway between two buildings, scaled a fence, cut across a yard, pushed his way through a thick hedge, and walked into a barn. Burke followed him and the Kid slid the door shut.

"Where are we?" asked Burke.

"My barn," said the Kid. "We're safe here unless Belle shows us." He grinned. "Sure taught those boys a lesson, eh, Burke?"

Burke took off his hat and eyed the ragged shot holes in it. "Yeh," he said quietly. "A *permanent* lesson." He cocked his head to listen to the hoarse shouting down the street as men gathered at the scene of the shooting "Who was the third *hombre?*"

"*Quien sabe?*"

"If we killed Harv and Curly, it's a cinch the third man must have been Larry Newman."

Jesse shoved back his hat. "Yeh," he said. "I wish to God I had gotten him too. He won't never rest now, Burke, until he gets me, and *you*, too, for that matter."

Burke slowly reloaded his Colt. It had been a near thing. If Curly had fired a few seconds faster he would have blown Jesse's head into bloody meat fragments, and quite possibly one of the other two drygulchers, or both, would have gotten in a killing shot or two at Burke.

Jesse reached inside his coat and withdrew a pint bottle. He handed it to Burke, and Burke took a neat slug of the warming contents. Jesse tipped up the bottle and drank deeply He lowered the bottle, wiped his mouth and then grinned. "By Godfrey," he said. "Nearly busted the bottle when you knocked me down. Thanks again, Burke. That's the third time you saved my life."

"We're even," said Burke quietly. "I saved you, and you saved me. Harv had me cold out there."

"They had the both of us cold," said Jesse. "We got more luck than brains."

"Now you know why I waited for you."

The Kid nodded, then eyed Burke closely. "I was wondering about that, *amigo*."

Burke did not look at him. Even in the darkness it was possible Jesse might see the cold and calculating look in Burke's icy blue eyes; the killing look. "I'm getting out of here," he said. "I'll cut along the next street, then come into the hotel by the back way. I've got to report to the ranch tomorrow, wherever that is."

"Don't worry. I'm going with you."

"Thanks. I can find it"

Jesse smiled. "It ain't that easy, Burke. Ben Hinch told me to make *sure* you got out there."

Burke turned. "What do you mean?"

"I happen to work for Ben Hinch, too, partner. *Remember?*"

Burke nodded. He eased open the door. "Seven o'clock," he said over his shoulder.

"Keno."

Burke faded into the darkness. He cut over to the next street, found it empty, hurried to the next intersection, then down the alleyway, luckily unseen. He saw men grouped about the body in the street and another group standing near the building. He remembered his slicker and walked quickly to the ramada where he had hidden it. His questing hands found nothing. A lighted match revealed that both slicker and rope had vanished. There was a cold feeling within him as he entered his hotel by the back way, and it didn't come from the cold wetness of the night, or the recent close bout with violent death in the street. His name was India-inked under the collar of that slicker.

He made it to his room without being seen, then stripped off his wet and muddy clothing. He wrapped a blanket about his lean, muscular body and looked down into the side street where two men had died in as many minutes. They were carrying the bodies up to the main street. Jesse Lester had used more sense in running from the scene of the killings than Burke had by wanting to stay there. Joe Moss had no longer been with the Hinch corrida when Burke had killed him, so it mattered not to Ben Hinch, but Curly Carter and the man named Harv had still been active in the corrida, and from what Burke had heard of Hinch's methods, he knew the big man did not tolerate gunplay within his private army.

Still, the third of the drygulchers had escaped. That, and the fact that Burke's slicker and the rawhide rope had mysteriously vanished during the night, was enough to warn Burke Dane that he was treading a little too heavily footed on eggs he could not afford to break. Poisonous eggs for Burke Dane.

The morning had dawned fresh and clear after the rain of the night. Cloud puffs drifted swiftly across the fresh and startling blue of the sky. The drying wind soughed through the trees as Burke Dane and Jesse Lester rode west from Piñon along the West Fork of the Rio Desperado on the way to Ben Hinch's Double Bar H spread.

"That is all Hinch land," said the Kid, as he waved an arm toward the land across the rushing river. "The best land in the Rio Desperado country, Burke. Good for cattle, timber and some mining. Ben has his fingers into every money making pie around here, I tell you."

Burke rolled a cigarette. "Hasn't anyone ever put up a fight against him?"

Jesse shrugged. "Now and then. Not as often as they used to. Used to be some pretty bloody fracases when Ben was on his way up, but he got the reins in his hands about five years ago and he hasn't let go of them. When he passes on, I wonder what Clete will do about handling the Hinch properties."

"What do you mean? Isn't Clete like his old man?"

Jesse accepted the makings from Burke. "In some ways," he said.

"Maybe it's the old story about the father making good, pulling himself up by his bootstraps to make a career for himself, only to realize he has to turn it over to a wastrel or weakling."

"This time the story is different, Burke. Clete is no wastrel and no weakling. His big trouble is he's already anxious to take over and the old man doesn't want to let go—*yet* anyways. Once in awhile the two of them go round and round, but the son ain't a big enough man to beat his old man's britches off, I tell you. He's biding his time."

"Is that why Belle is going with Clete?"

The Kid turned slowly to look directly at Burke. "I don't like that kind of talk, Burke."

"Sorry."

Jesse nodded and lighted his cigarette. "Well, anyway I can't really blame her, Burke. We haven't got a red cent Hellsfire! I owe every merchant in town, seems like. Sure, there are plenty of other men camping on Belle's hocks, waiting for a chance with her, legal or otherwise, but Belle is smart. 'Shoot for ducks' is her motto. Clete Hinch will be the big man in this country some day and I guess Belle figures she might as well be Mrs. Big as anything else around here."

Burke blew out a puff of smoke. "Well, I have a feeling Belle won't be any tame kitten for a man to have around, even if he *is* Mister Big."

"Keno." Jesse pointed ahead. "There's the ranch now, beyond that timber."

A heavy long bridge spanned the Rio

Desperado and beyond it, through the timber, Burke saw a mass of buildings, white-washed, shining in the bright morning sun. Several windmills whirred in the freshening wind. It was quite a spread; in fact a whale of a spread, thought Burke. It smelled of profit and wealth, and yet there was nothing ostentatious about the place. Its size and layout indicated money, rather than any useless and materialistic trappings.

"Ben keeps adding on," said Jesse as they crossed the bridge. "Any new ideas, tools, blood stock, all end up here, but not for show, I tell you. Ben bleeds money out of everything he gets his hands on, or out it goes."

"Like his gunfighters?"

Jesse looked sideways at Burke. "You're getting the idea fast, *amigo*," he said dryly.

"What happens when a man doesn't measure up?"

Jesse jerked a thumb toward the distant mountains. "He leaves thataway."

"Or gets buried on Hinch land, is that it?"

Jesse spat into the clear water. "Well, Ben don't charge the deceased's family for the burial plot, if that's what you're driving at. Hawww!"

"You're coming out with a good one now and then," said Burke. He flipped his cigarette butt into the river.

Jesse turned in his saddle. "One thing, Burke: Ben usually requires a new man to prove himself."

"Meaning?"

The Kid's face was expressionless. "A man has to blood himself to prove he rates riding with the Hinch corrida."

"You mean a killing?"

Jesse smiled. "You're getting the idea."

"So Ben has something to hold over his head, is that it?"

"Yes."

Burke shrugged. "I've got two killings against me already. In Piñon at any rate."

"Joe Moss doesn't count. Besides, if Ben knows we killed Curly Carter and Harv last night he won't take it lightly."

"You think that third man will talk?"

"I'm banking he won't. Those three boys weren't waiting for us on Ben's orders, you can bet your boots on that. Ben don't allow any fighting within the corrida. If that third man is one of Ben's men, he won't likely open his mouth."

"And if he isn't?"

The Kid smiled quickly. "Then what difference does it make? He sure as hell ain't going to go around blowing about how he was a party in an attempt to drygulch two of Hinch's boys, is he?"

"You've got something there," said Burke. The thought of the missing slicker and rope fled through his mind. He'd have to sweat that out. It wasn't yet time for him to make any moves.

A tall man came striding from the big ranchhouse as Jesse and Burke drew rein and dismounted. "Jesse!" he called out. "Mount again! We've got work to do! Who's that with you?"

"Burke Dane, Clete," said Jesse.

The man swung up into the saddle of

a fine black. "The new man? Good! We can use another man."

"What's up?" asked Jesse as he mounted.

"Trouble over in the meadow country. The rest of the boys are busy up north. It's up to you and me, and Dane as well. We'll meet Larry Newman at the line shack by Cold Creek."

"Dandy," said Jesse out of the side of his mouth. "If that *was* Larry who got away last night, he'll be sporting a bullet scratch somewhere, or I miss my guess."

Clete Hinch rode toward them. Burke was struck by his resemblance to his father, although he was a taller and better looking man. Clete eyed Burke up and down. "My father said you were a good man with a gun. Is that right?"

"I can take care of myself, Clete," said Burke quietly.

"You call me mister Hinch, Dane. Understand?"

Burke nodded and looked at Jesse. Jesse smiled. "Likely Clete and me will

110

be brother-in-laws some day. Clete *allows* me to call him by his first name."

Clete shot an angry glance at Jesse. "I swear to God, Kid, you go too far sometimes!"

Jesse's expression changed. "What's the trouble you spoke about, Clete?"

"Sticky loopers. Larry sent one of the boys back to say he had seen three or four of them working in the timber over against Bald Mountain."

"A good place," said Jesse. "Can't see very far in that timber. They can cut out a few head of cows and run them up a canyon until dark, then edge them along the base of the mountain until it gets daylight, run them up into another canyon until dark, and so on."

"We'll take care of that this time," said Clete. He smashed a gloved hand down on his saddle horn. "I hope to God we catch 'em cold this time."

Burke rolled another cigarette. "What happens then?" he asked.

Clete looked at him. "We don't give

rustlers a second chance in the Rio Desperado country."

"A law unto yourselves, is that it?" asked Burke.

Hinch stared at him. "What the hell do you mean by that?"

Burke smiled. "I heard you gave short shrift to rustlers over here."

"Where do you come from?"

"New Mexico."

"*Where* in New Mexico?"

"All over, Mister Hinch."

"One of that kind, eh?"

Burke nodded. "One of that kind, Mister Hinch."

"You said the Big Bonito country once," said Jesse.

Clete Hinch shot another glance at Burke. "Is that right, Dane?"

Burke shrugged. "I worked around there while drifting west, is all."

"Know a man named Print Campbell?"

Once again Dane's poker training kept his face impassive. "I've heard of him."

"Charley Mayo?"

It wasn't easy this time for Burke. "I've heard of him," he said casually. "Rancher, isn't he?"

"Was," said Jesse. He grinned.

Burke lighted his cigarette, trying hard to keep control. "Was? What happened to him?"

Clete splashed his black through a rivulet. "Seems as though Charley Mayo was a son-in-law to Print Campbell, Dane."

"So?"

They all reached the far bank of the rivulet. "Mayo got a little out of hand over here not too long ago," said Clete.

"And?"

Clete turned. "I said we didn't give rustlers a second chance in this country."

"There's Larry," said Jesse quickly. He looked at Burke. "Somebody strung Mayo up in Windy Pass. Sort of a warning you might say. We don't cotton to New Mexico men coming over here and stealing Arizona cattle, *amigo*."

"You had the goods on Mayo then?" asked Burke quietly.

Clete forced the black up a cutbank. He turned and looked at Burke. "We never said *we* did the hanging," he said. "But Print Campbell was run out of here long ago, and told to stay away from here."

"Was Mayo hung because he was a rustler or because he was a son-in-law of Print Campbell?" asked Burke.

"What the hell difference does it make?" said Clete.

"None, I guess," said Burke.

Jesse Lester eyed Burke quickly, and an odd expression fled across his handsome face.

Larry Newman was sitting easily in his saddle, a leg hooked around the horn, a cigarette dangling from his lips. He nodded shortly as the three riders approached and drew rein. There was no sign of a wound about the tall man, but Jesse could have scratched his hide somewhere with a bullet and the wound could be well hidden.

"What's up?" asked Clete.

Larry flipped away his cigarette.

"They're still over there," he said, jerking his head toward a huge outthrust shoulder of the towering mountain of almost naked rock. "I've been keeping an eye on them all morning."

"Bold as brass, eh?" said Clete. "In broad daylight."

"They had a lookout," said Larry casually. "I took care of him. They probably still think he's keepin' an eye out for some of our boys."

"Good work, Larry," said Clete. "Lead the way!" He eased his Winchester in its saddle scabbard. "I hope to God we can trap *all* of them!"

Burke eyed the rancher. There was a cold eagerness on Hinch's face that boded no good for the sticky loopers.

The four of them rode toward the thick timber; death in the saddle.

6

THE three rustlers were working fast, driving twenty head along the wide meadowland toward the thick timber that edged the mountain base. Although it was hard to tell exactly where the canyon opening was against the masses of eroded and splintered rock of the great talus slope, it was obvious that the sticky loopers knew where it was, for they moved confidently toward the timber that shielded the canyon mouth.

"That's all of them," said Newman.

"You're sure?" asked Clete Hinch.

Larry turned a little and there was almost a sarcastic smile on his lean hard face. "No chance of us getting dry-gulched, if that's what you mean, Mister Hinch."

"I wasn't thinking of that," said Clete quickly. "I want all of them. *All*, you understand?" He shot hard looks at his gunfighters.

Jesse shoved back his hat. "Me and Burke can cut along the east side of the meadows. The ground is lower there and hidden by timber. We can get to the canyon mouth before they do."

Clete nodded. "Go on then. Larry and me will keep to the west, and close in on them if they break back this way."

Jesse set the steel to his bay and rode swiftly to the east, followed by Burke. Burke looked back to see Clete and Larry drawing out their rifles. Then the two of them rode into the timber.

It was a beautiful day. Birds twittered in the timber. Patches of sunlight moved back and forth in the dappled shade. A deer moved silently and swiftly across a glade and disappeared into the woods. A porcupine stood in the trail and did not move as the two horsemen approached him. "Spunky buggers, ain't they?" asked Jesse. He spat at the bristly creature.

It was easy. Burke and Jesse tethered their horses in the timber, took their rifles, and padded quickly through the timber to where they could see the narrow canyon mouth. They reached the area ten minutes before the rustlers. The cattle bawled hoarsely. Now and then the rustlers looked nervously over their shoulders toward the creek in the distance. They hadn't been warned of the approach of the Double Bar H men and they never would be, for the first of them was already dead in the timber.

Jesse shoved back his hat and levered a round into his Winchester. "You any good with the long gun?" he asked casually.

"Fair."

The cattle were now even with Jesse and Burke, and the three drivers were too intent on their work to watch for anyone. Jesse quickly raised his rifle and fired. The sharp report rang up the canyon and the horse of the lead driver went down. The rustler leaped free and ran toward the timber but Jesse had reloaded. He swung the rifle easily and just as he fired, Burke bumped purposely against him.

The man staggered as the slug hit him and went down writhing on the damp ground.

The gunsmoke drifted through the timber. The other two rustlers lashed their mounts, trying to reach the canyon, then saw Burke and Jesse mounting their horses. They turned and raced back along the meadow. A rifle spoke flatly and the lead rider pitched heavily from the saddle while his horse veered off and ran toward Jesse and Burke. The third and last rustler turned his horse and drew out a pistol. He fired wildly at Jesse and Burke. Two rifles cracked together from the west side of the meadow and the rider stiffened in the saddle, then fell sideways, his foot caught in the stirrup. The horse galloped toward the bawling cattle, dragging his rider behind him. The horse vanished in the canyon mouth along with the cattle.

The smoke drifted slowly across that meadow of death. Jesse looked at Burke. "You bump me apurpose?" he asked.

"Maybe. You were going to kill him, weren't you?"

"I didn't see *you* do any shooting."

"I thought he wanted them captured."

Jesse slid his rifle into its sheath. "Sometimes you ain't too bright, *amigo*."

"They got three out of four and saved the cattle. Isn't that enough?"

Jesse rolled a cigarette and shook his head. "Not for Clete Hinch, it ain't. Come on. The second act is about to begin."

Clete and Larry had stopped at the still figure of the man lying in the middle of the meadow. Larry dismounted and hooked a foot under the man, heaving him over on his back. His arms were outflung. Larry looked up at Clete and nodded. The two of them rode toward the wounded man. The four horsemen met together, sitting easily in their saddles, looking down on the sweat damp face of the kid, for he was hardly more than that. His clawed hands ripped steadily at his left shoulder.

"You're getting out of practice, Kid," said Larry.

Jesse spat. "Any time you want a match, Larry, you just say so."

Larry looked at Burke. "No score for the 'Man from New Mexico,' eh?"

"He doesn't know the rules yet," said Jesse.

"He better, by God, learn the rules, and pronto!" snapped Clete.

Burke dismounted and ground-reined his horse. He walked toward the kid on the ground and knelt beside him.

"What the hell!" said Larry.

Burke took the Colt from the kid's holster and tossed it to one side. "Let me take a look at that wound," he said.

"Get up, Dane," said Clete Hinch.

Burke ignored him as he began to free the bloody shirt from the wound.

"Get up, *you*," said Clete once more.

Burke had exposed the wound. He eased the kid back onto the ground. A gun hammer clicked back. Burke looked up into the stoney eyes of Clete Hinch and the one cold, black eye of a gun muzzle. "He'll bleed to death, Mister Hinch," he said quietly.

"Up, damn you!"

Burke wiped the blood from his hands and stood up.

"Get that horse, Larry," said Hinch.

The gunfighter rode toward the stray. He led it back toward the waiting men. "Mount," said Clete to the kid.

Sweat trickled down the rustler's face. He got weakly to his feet and fell against the horse. The horse shied and blew at the smell of fresh blood.

"Mount!" snapped Clete Hinch.

The kid got a boot into the stirrup but he couldn't make it into the saddle.

"He can't ride," said Burke harshly to Hinch. "Let me bandage him and take him up in front of me, Mister Hinch."

"Jesse said you didn't know the rules," said the rancher. "Help him, Larry."

Larry pulled the kid roughly up until he could fork the horse and grip the saddlehorn. He looked at Burke. "My name is Jerry Kenna," he said. "From Benson. My maw lives there."

Burke looked curiously at him.

"Now!" yelled Clete.

Larry lashed the kid's horse over the rump with his reins. The horse galloped toward the canyon mouth. Jesse and Larry looked at Clete. "Let Burke have him," said the rancher. He looked at Burke.

"*You* go to hell, *Mister* Hinch," said Burke Dane. "And none of *you* try to get that kid!" It was then he realized that Clete Hinch still held a sixgun aimed at him.

Jesse raised his rifle and looked at Larry. "Ten bucks I get the hoss" His rifle cracked and the horse staggered in its stride. Larry's rifle spoke but he missed. Jesse fired again. The horse went down and the kid fell heavily. He staggered to his feet and looked wildly about, then began a slow run toward the timber. Jesse raised his rifle but Larry Newman beat him to the punch. The Winchester rang out and the kid went down with a slug between the shoulder blades.

Again the powdersmoke drifted across the quiet meadow as the gunshot echoes died away. Now Burke knew why the kid had told him his name and home. The kid knew more about these men of the Double Bar H than Burke knew. He knew he was doomed.

Clete let down the hammer on his Colt. "You've got a lot to learn, Dane," he said. "I should fire you right now."

"You didn't hire me, Mister Hinch," said Burke evenly. "It's up to your father to fire me."

"I can take it upon myself to fire you!" snapped the rancher.

"Go on then," said Burke easily. "Do that, Mister Hinch."

For a long moment there was pure hell in the man's eyes and his lips worked.

"There's Belle, Clete," said Jesse quickly.

Clete turned in the saddle and saw the lovely young woman riding toward them. "I don't want her to see this mess," he said. He spurred his black toward her.

"Gentle soul, ain't he?" said Burke.

"You work for the Double Bar H, Dane, and you obey the rules," said Newman.

"I don't believe in killing helpless men," said Burke.

"Seems as though you change the rules to suit yourself, eh, Dane?"

Burke eyed the gunfighter. "I can kill when I have to, Newman. You ought to know that."

"Your day will come, Dane." Larry Newman kneed his horse away from the two of them and rode toward the canyon. "We can't get those cows back sitting here talking," he said over his shoulder.

Jesse shook his head as he and Burke rode after Larry. "You're all horns, hoofs and rattles this morning," he said to Burke. "Beats me." He looked back toward Clete. "So help me. You could'a got away with what you said to Ben Hinch, because Ben Hinch, for all his money grabbing and lust for power, secretly admires a man who stands up against him, *if* that man is right."

Burke rolled a cigarette. "Maybe a man like Print Campbell or Charley Mayo, eh?"

Jesse's eyes narrowed. "Why did you say that?"

"I've heard stories. Print Campbell was blinded apurpose, wasn't he?"

"That was before my time on the Double Bar H. Just what the hell do you know about Charley Mayo?"

"Rumors, Kid, only rumors. Let's go get those cows!"

Jesse hesitated, watching Burke galloping toward the canyon mouth, and his sister's words came back to him on the wind soughing through the pines. *"He isn't any run of the mill saddle tramp. There is something secret about that man."* And again: *"And this man, this Burke Dane, from nowhere, drew and killed him when Joe had his gun out and cocked?"*

An uneasy feeling fled through the cocky young mind of Jesse Lester, and he remembered too that very morning, in the dark and wet, when Burke Dane had seen Curly Carter hiding in the ruins with a scattergun in his hands and had saved Jesse's life by driving him to one side.

Jesse hadn't seen anything. Jesse owed Dane his life, not once, but maybe three times: first in the pass; then when he had killed Joe Moss; thirdly, when he had saved Jesse from Curly Carter.

He liked and admired Burke Dane, but now something else had crept into his mind. It was a tried and true saying that there was always a better man than you somewhere in the wide world, and that it was inevitable that you would meet him for a showdown. For the first time in his careless young life, Jesse Lester felt the weight of being known as a fast gun and a gunfighter. Such a reputation had to be maintained at any cost. Such a reputation bred enemies; men who only wanted to beat you to prove to the world that they were the fastest gun. These men came from nowhere. Maybe from California or Utah; Colorado or Texas; *or New Mexico* . . .

It took several hours to round up the spooked cattle. They had found the body of the third rustler up the canyon, his head battered beyond recognition from beating against the rocks as he was dragged by his horse. They drove the cattle back into the meadow, and while Larry stood guard, Jesse and Burke hauled the bodies to the canyon and buried them in a deep rock cleft, filling the cleft with detritus and loose rock.

Everything went with them. Guns and saddles were pitched in. It was Ben Hinch's way. Let their friends and relatives wonder what had happened to the four men who had taken their guts into their dirty hands to rustle cattle from the Double Bar H. The fact that they did not return, and no traces would ever be found of them, made the reputation of Ben Hinch and the Double Bar H corrida just that much more omnipotent and sinister.

7

THE sun was in its zenith when Jesse and Burke rode back to the headquarters of the Double Bar H. Larry Newman had left ahead of them, for he was ramrod under Matt Foxx, and there were other things for him to do. "I wonder if it was him this morning," said Jesse thoughtfully.

"He didn't show any signs of being wounded, Kid. Unless you missed him."

"I can call my shots," said Jesse carelessly. He eyed Burke. "I'd still like to know if it *was* him."

"We can try to find out," said Burke. "What do we do if he was the third man?"

"We'll know how far he'll go to even up the score, *amigo*."

"I think we both know that already."

"Well, no one else but us besides that third man knows who killed Harv and

Curly. We keep our mouths shut and play dumb, which shouldn't be too hard for you, and that third man might make his slip."

"Then what?"

Jesse sneered like a hunting lobo wolf. "We'll have to teach that jasper a lesson he won't forget."

A man came out of the main building and looked at the two of them. "Mister Hinch wants to see you two in the house, Jesse," he called out. "Pronto!"

"Which Mister Hinch, Shorty?" asked Jesse as he dismounted.

"The Big Man, Jesse."

Jesse shrugged. "Wonder what the hell is wrong now," he said in an aside to Burke.

"*Quien sabe?* I haven't got anything to hide."

Jesse's eyes went wide. "You haven't?" he asked in mock surprise. He turned and walked toward the big house.

Burke flipped away his cigarette and eyed the Kid as he followed him toward the house. Jesse was as sharp as a Barlow knife, under all his assumed nonchalance and carelessness. Burke was beginning to wonder just how much Jesse knew.

Ben Hinch had furnished his big house well, though nothing in it was ostentatious. Burke nodded as the two of them waited in the large living room. It was just such a way he himself would have furnished such a room, if he had the means. It was comfortable enough, but yet, to Burke, there was a haunting coldness about the place.

Ben Hinch walked into the room and sat down near the fireplace. He eyed the two of them. "Larry Newman said you did all right this morning, Jesse. That doesn't surprise me. I heard differently about your friend there."

"He doesn't know the rules, Mister Hinch," said Jesse.

"Well, Dane, what do you have to say for yourself?" asked the rancher.

"I don't know all the rules, Mister Hinch. But I do know you suffered no losses this morning, in cattle or men, and there are four rustlers buried up the canyon. Considering this is my first day of work for you, I can see no cause for complaint."

"You talk like a shyster lawyer," growled Hinch. "One thing worse than an ignorant cowpoke is a smart one, or one who *thinks* he's smart. Which one are you?

Burke smiled. "I've read a little law, Mister Hinch."

Hinch leaned back in his chair and lighted a cigar. "No matter about this morning. You did well enough, but next time don't be so squeamish. I've lost at least four men in the past few years, shot to death by rustlers. This is war in this country, Dane. I have the finest cattle in this entire area, and I mean to keep them, one way or another. That's why I keep the corrida I have. That is why I need men like you, and Jesse there. Don't worry about being brought to account for killing those human vermin. *I* take care of my men, legally or otherwise."

"Do you take care of their consciences too, Mister Hinch?" asked Burke quietly.

"Oh Lord," said Jesse. He rolled his eyes upward.

For a long moment Ben Hinch studied Burke. "The men I hire, Mister Dane, may have consciences, but those consciences are not active after such killings like those of this morning. There is a difference between justice and softness in this country."

"I almost forgot where I was," said Burke.

Hinch blew out a puff of smoke. "You'll learn. Now, let's get on to other matters. Two of my men were shot to death on the streets of Piñon early this morning. Harv Clayton and Curly Carter. The killers, and there are thought to be two of them, escaped. There were no witnesses. I've already sent my son Clete into Piñon to make an investigation. Matt Foxx, as deputy-sheriff of this county will deputize Clete to make it legal."

Very neat, thought Burke. The fact that Ben Hinch was pushing an investigation, outwardly legal, though manipulated by Hinch himself, might prove that the man thought someone outside the Hinch corrida had killed two of his men. He couldn't and wouldn't allow that. It was against his principles, and Ben Hinch, in order to keep the reins tight in the Rio Desperado country, would have to see that those killers were brought to justice. What would happen if he found out that Jesse Lester and Burke Dane had killed those two men? What if the third man talked?

Hinch relighted his cigar. "I want Clete to learn the ways of the law," he said.

Like his Pappy, thought Burke.

Ben Hinch waved out the match flame. "A man has to know the law to keep in the saddle. The parts that protect him, and the loopholes, so that he doesn't get snarled himself." Hinch smiled. "You, as a student of law, Mister Dane, can hardly disagree with that theory."

"No, sir," said Burke.

Hinch stood up and walked to the fireplace. He flicked an ash from his cigar into the fireplace, then turned suddenly.

"Just what do you two men know about those killings this morning?" he spat out.

Jesse smiled, like the innocent child he usually portrayed at such times. "Nothing, Mister Hinch. Why do you ask?"

Hinch thrust his cigar into his mouth and worked it back and forth from one side to the other. "From the circumstances, it looked as though Curly Carter, at least, was lying in wait for someone. Harv Clayton was found dead in the street. Although no witnesses actually saw the shooting, they heard voices calling out, the voices of two men other than Curly and Harv."

"How did they place the number at two?" asked Jesse easily.

"Because those two men spoke to each other *after* Curly and Harv were shot to death. A third man was evidently shot at and escaped from the killers by riding from Piñon." Hinch's cold eyes darted back and forth between the two men. "Both of you were in Piñon last night. Both of you left the Hinch Hotel Bar

135

shortly before the shooting. From what I know about you, Jesse, and from Burke's shooting of Joe Moss in the Mecca yesterday morning, I would almost be willing to bet the pair of you could shoot your way out of most ambushes, and be able to cut a few new notches on the handles of your cutters after the shooting."

"Are you accusing us of killing those two men, Mister Hinch?" asked Burke.

"No. But *did* you?"

"No," lied Burke. "I heard the shooting as I entered my room in the Piñon Hotel. It was dark and it was raining. I could see very little from my window."

"And *you*, Jesse?" asked Hinch quickly.

Before the Kid could speak Burke broke in. "Jesse was pretty damned drunk last night, Mister Hinch. I had taken him home before I returned to my room."

"Very neat," said the rancher. "No witnesses either, eh?"

"My sister Belle," said Jesse. He smiled. "Belle always likes to tuck me in, Mister Hinch."

For a moment the man's face whitened in quick anger and then he smiled. "Fair enough! I won't press the matter. I happen to know Curly Carter was a good friend of Joe Moss'. Harv Clayton was Curly's sidekick. It would be like him to back Curly's play."

"That just leaves the man who escaped, as you tell the story, Mister Hinch," said Burke.

Ben Hinch threw his cigar into the fireplace. "Yes." He eyed Burke. "I can't bring those two men back to life. They weren't obeying any instructions of mine this morning. They paid the price for what they attempted." He walked to the table and selected another cigar. "Now get out of here! Take the rest of the day off. If I need you I'll send for you. In a few days I'll have a big job for you, and Dane, *this time you obey the rules. Comprende?*"

When they reached their horses Jesse

blew out an explosive breath. "Chihuahua! The old vinegaroon stings, doesn't he?"

Burke rolled a cigarette and looked back toward the house. "He knows," he said quietly.

"What makes you think so, Burke?"

"It's his business to know everything that is going on around the Rio Desperado country. That's how he stays on top, isn't it?"

"It doesn't make sense to me, Burke."

Burke mounted and rode toward the bridge, followed by Jesse. Burke looked back at Jesse. "I wonder if he put Curly and Harv up to that ambush?"

"You're loco!"

Burke shrugged. "Did you ever get the thought through your thick head that maybe Ben Hinch doesn't exactly *want* you around? That he has used you and wants no more part of you?"

"What the hell are you talking about?" demanded the Kid angrily.

"Maybe he wants you out of the way, Kid. He could have used the death of Joe

Moss to his advantage, by putting those men up to killing you."

"But you were there, too!"

"Exactly! Curly would have gotten the first one of us, and Harv and that third man the second of us, in less time than it takes to tell about it. Hinch didn't give a damn about Joe Moss."

"If he wants to get rid of me all he has to do is say so!"

Burke crossed the bridge and turned toward the road that led to Piñon. "You've forgotten one thing: Clete Hinch and Belle, Jesse. Clete isn't going to let his father get rid of you his usual way, not as long as Clete has his eyes on Belle."

Jesse rode up beside Burke and shot an uneasy glance at him. "But if I was shot down in the street by unknowns, it would sure serve the purpose wouldn't it?"

"You're getting the idea."

A slight shiver seemed to pass through the Kid. He turned in the saddle and looked back at the ranch. "I have one more thought on it, Burke."

"Yes?"

Jesse turned again. "Maybe Ben Hinch didn't know a thing about the ambush, like he said. Maybe it was *Clete's* idea. I wouldn't put it past him."

"Whoever thought it up, it was a damned close thing."

Jesse eyed Burke. "And where do you fit in, Man of New Mexico? Seems to me, if I had wandered into this country like you did, and got belly deep in trouble the first twenty-four hours I was here, I'd been long gone."

"I got a job, Kid," said Burke.

"Yeh, you got a job all right. You almost got measured for a nice new pine suit with brass handles on it too."

Neither of them had much to say for the rest of the ride into Piñon, but every now and then Jesse would glance surreptitiously at the hawkface of the man riding beside him. As they entered the town Burke looked at the Kid. "What kind of trouble did Charley Mayo get into over here, Kid?" he asked.

Jesse's eyes narrowed. "Why do you ask?"

"Clete Hinch said he was a son-in-law to Print Campbell. I knew Print years ago. Print was a tough cob in the old days. I heard a story once that it was Ben Hinch who had Print blinded. Broke Print's spirit, from what I heard."

"You sure heard a helluva lot, didn't you?"

Burke swung down at the street corner and looked up at the Kid. "You mean to tell me the Hinches strung up Charley Mayo simply because he was son-in-law to Print?"

The Kid's face worked a little. "No."

"Was Mayo really a rustler, Kid?"

Jesse shoved back his hat. "I don't know. Mayo came over here to buy cattle from Ben Hinch. Ben has the best cattle to be had and his prices ain't *too* high, if a man wants them bad enough."

"So?"

Jesse shrugged. "Mayo was a good hand with the cards. Got into a big game at the Hinch Hotel. I started out in the game, but it got too rich for me. Mayo was taking pot after pot. Never seen anything like it. I swear he was ahead five thousand dollars by the time the game broke up."

Burke rolled a cigarette. He glanced down the street and saw Belle Lester standing at the gate of the little house, not far beyond the place where Curly Carter and Harv Clayton had died in a hurry early that very morning.

Jesse dismounted and took the makings from Burke's hand. He began to fashion a quirly. "Mayo said he had enough money to buy a helluva lot more cows from Ben Hinch. Never seen a man so excited. He was calm as an oyster during the tightest parts of the game, but when it was over, and he got to talking about buying them cattle, he reminded me of a kid eyeing his bulgin' Christmas stocking."

Burke lighted up and held the cupped match to light Jesse's cigarette. The Kid had known Charley all right. Charley was a cool man with the cards, damned near as good as Burke at his best. But when it came to cattle, Charley was actually like the kid Jesse had likened him to. It was almost an obsession with Charley. It was something Burke had not shared with him.

Jesse blew a perfect smoke ring. "Well, Charley headed out, all right. Hired a couple of boys to give him a hand when he got the cows. Needed hands to get them over Windy Pass and over to the Big Bonito country. You know the rest of the story." Jesse spat. "Charley Mayo was strung up for a sticky looper."

"Was he guilty?"

"*Quien sabe?*"

"With five thousand dollars in his hands, why would he steal cattle, especially when he knew the reputation of Ben Hinch for dealing with rustlers? It doesn't make sense!"

Jesse took the cigarette from his mouth. "I didn't tell you who was the big loser in that poker game."

"Go on."

The Kid's eyes held Burke's. "It was Clete Hinch."

A cold feeling crept over Burke. Pieces

of the puzzle were slowly fitting into place. "Did Mayo get his cattle?" he asked quietly.

"Yes."

"Where are they?"

Jesse smiled. "He was hung for a rustler, wasn't he?"

Burke's eyes narrowed. "So he loses his cattle, his winnings and his life."

"You're getting the idea, Burke."

"Who were the men he hired to help him?"

Jesse flipped away his cigarette. He took the reins of his horse. "Got to see Belle," he said. "See you later, Burke." He walked a few paces and then turned. "Don't ask so damned many questions around Pinon, *amigo*. 'Person might get suspicious. Ain't everyone around here like *me*, Burke. Keep that in mind. *Adios!*"

"*Adios!*" Burke watched the Kid walk toward his house, softly whistling, right past the place where he had killed Harv Clayton. Burke led his horse to the livery stable, then went to his room to clean up.

Jesse Lester's story about the last days of Charley Mayo had come as a shocking revelation to Burke. It was true that Ben Hinch was a hard and unscrupulous man, not averse to force and killings, but he was also a businessman. He had bred the finest cattle in that country for that purpose. Why would he have a man like Charley Mayo put to a degrading death when the New Mexico rancher had money and the wish to buy cattle from Hinch? It didn't make sense to Burke.

He dug out a bottle and poured a stiff drink. He paced back and forth in his room, smoking and trying to form a clearer picture of the tangled situation. His mission had gotten out of control. It seemed to take a way of its own, despite what he wanted to do. It had all started with his saving Jesse Lester in Windy Pass, and from then on he seemed to have become the tool of the fates, who were probably laughing toothlessly at the poor thing called man they had trapped in their meshes.

Things that had been said to him drifted into his mind.

Clete is no wastrel and no weakling. His big trouble is he's already anxious to take over and the old man doesn't want to let go—yet anyways. Once in awhile the two of them go round and round, but the son ain't a big enough man to beat his old man's britches off, I tell you. He's biding his time . . .

He sipped his drink. "Charley didn't antagonize Ben Hinch," he said aloud. "It was Clete Hinch he antagonized. It was Clete who took the beating in that poker game. Why would Ben want to lynch a man like Charley? Sure, he'd lynch a real rustler and think nothing of it, but if a man came to him with five thousand dollars, wanting to buy cattle, Ben Hinch would become the legal businessman, not the avenging lyncher of a man who had never given him cause for stringing him up."

If it was Clete Hinch who had seen to it that Charley was lynched, he didn't do it alone, *and it was Jesse Lester's rope*

146

that did the job. The rope that was taken from where Burke had hidden it. The thought made him put on his hat and coat, and leave the cheerless room. If Jesse Lester had been one of the lynchers, and he found out that his treasured rawhide rope had been found wrapped in the slicker of a man named Burke Dane, all the Kid's suspicions would come to a head, and Burke wasn't at all sure he could beat Jesse Lester to the draw.

Burke Dane now had three objectives in mind. He was quite sure it would be impossible to get all the men who had been party to the merciless lynching of Charley Mayo. Therefore he would cut it down to the *one* man who had been responsible. The man who had given the order that had been the last words Charley Mayo had heard on this troubled earth. The second objective was to find out who had the five thousand dollars Charley had won in that poker game. That, at least, was the due of Marion Mayo and her two children.

The third and last objective was, for

Burke Dane, after getting the man responsible for Charley's death and collecting the missing five thousand dollars, to get out of the Rio Desperado Valley with a whole skin. That, thought Burke, would likely be the toughest objective of the three. He remembered his last brave words to Print Campbell: "I'll ram my navel into the sand trying!" They echoed hollowly enough now.

8

IT was dusk when Burke Dane convinced himself that finding his slicker and the incriminating rawhide rope that belonged to Jesse Lester was an impossible task. During his secretive search for both articles he studied Piñon and its people, knowing full well that the people of Piñon were also studying him. It's easy enough for a man to vanish, almost without trace in a big city, or out on the open plains, or in the mountain country, but no one can escape scrutiny, interest and downright suspicion in a small town such as Piñon; particularly when a man is stamped in the mold of Burke Dane.

An uneasy feeling had come to roost in Burke's mind. Every fiber of his body seemed to have an almost uncontrollable itch for Burke to light a shuck out of Piñon and the Rio Desperado country and stand not upon the way of his going.

His association with Jesse Lester had started the ball rolling and his swift and efficient killing of Joe Moss had accelerated the speed of the ball. No one knew for sure, of course, that Burke Dane was one of the two men who peddled out sudden death to Harv Clayton and Curly Carter. To Burke, whose mind always seemed to work with amazing clarity in times of stress and danger, the danger signals were flying.

He did not delude himself into believing he was accepted as another gunslick of the feared and powerful Double Bar H corrida, and amongst their ranks he had already many dangerous enemies. Ben Hinch himself certainly had not as yet accepted Burke Dane at face value. Ben Hinch had not risen to wealth and power by being a snap judge of men.

There was a little pattering of rain upon the leaves of the trees as Burke stood on the bridge looking down into the dark waters of the river, at the eastern limits of Piñon, and it brought to mind the fact that he did not have a slicker. He rolled a cigarette and walked back up the main street until he saw a secondhand clothing store He entered and looked about for a clerk.

A baldheaded man looked up from a sewing machine at the back of the dimly lighted shop. "Can I help you?" he asked.

"I need a slicker," said Burke.

The man nodded and stood up. "New or used?" he asked.

"New."

Again the man nodded. He eyed Burke's build and then took a slicker from a rack "New goods," he said with a smile. Then he peered more closely at Burke and his face changed a little.

"Anything wrong?" asked Burke as he tried on the slicker.

"Not exactly, Mister Dane."

Burke eyed him quickly. "What do you mean?"

"You're buying this slicker because you lost your old one?"

"I wouldn't be buying a new slicker if I already had one, would I, Mister?"

The man flushed. He looked toward the back of the shop. It was then that Burke noted the material the man had been working on at the sewing machine. It was yellow slicker material. Burke took off the new slicker and walked back to the machine. He turned back the collar of the slicker and saw his name neatly printed on it with India ink. "Where did you get this?" he asked over his shoulder.

"I deal in second hand goods, Mister Dane. A man brought that in. I bought it for a few dollars and was repairing it when I saw your name. I intended to let you know I had it, then charge you for the repair work."

Burke nodded. "Fair enough." He turned. "Who brought it in?"

The man hesitated. He glanced toward the front door.

"Come on," said Burke quietly. "I'm buying the new slicker anyway."

"Man by name of Benny Peak. He's the town drunk, Mister Dane. You won't cause him any trouble, will you? Benny didn't mean any harm."

"I just want to talk with him," said Burke.

"Something missing?"

"In a way."

The man came closer to Burke. "Benny hangs out in Garvey's place when he has money." He smiled. "Probably drank up what I paid him for the slicker already."

"I'll reimburse you."

"Thanks." The man handed Burke the new slicker. "You want me to wrap up the old one?"

Burke nodded. He put on the new slicker, paid the man, and took the wrapped slicker.

The man glanced again at the front door. "Happens there was something else with the slicker, Mister Dane. A rawhide reata, Benny said. One of the best he had ever seen. He said he'd get enough for it to keep him going for two days. Lots of men around here would pay plenty for a rope like the one he found, he said. Was it yours, Mister Dane?"

Burke rolled a cigarette. "In a way."

The man's dark eyes studied him. "You don't have to worry about me," he said. "I hate the guts of the men who run this country. I got no use for any of them. Well, we got a good start this week. Three of them gone. Joe Moss, Harv Clayton and Curly Carter. Keep going, Mister Dane."

Burke was repelled by the hard look in the man's eyes, but he had to take a chance on the man. "Keep your mouth shut about me coming in here, you understand?"

"I don't know anything."

Burke walked to the door.

"Garvey's place, Mister Dane," called out the man. "He's probably there right now. Only got one eye. You can't miss him."

Dane turned up the collar of the new slicker as he stepped outside to face a chilly drizzle. It was an off-and-on rainy season in the high country this time of year. He walked up the street and into the livery stable where he kept his dun.

154

He placed the old slicker in one of his saddlebags and then went on to Garvey's saloon. He peered through the dirty, rain streaked window. There were several men in the place. From where he was it was impossible to see if a one-eyed man was one of them.

He walked in and nodded to Garvey. "Beer," he said.

"Wet night, Mister Dane."

Burke nodded. He glanced down the bar. None of the three men standing there were familiar to him. None of them were one-eyed. A drunk sat at a rear table, head back against the wall, mouth agape, snoring loudly. Burke sipped his beer, then walked toward the back of the place. There was a newspaper on the table next to where the drunk slept. Burke picked it up, then surreptitiously kicked the ankle of the man. He choked and snapped open his bleary eyes. "What the hell!" he said. Bleary as his eyes were, they were both there.

"Sorry," said Burke. He walked back

to his beer. "Wrong paper," he said casually to Garvey.

"Only one we got."

Burke sipped at his beer. He was faced with the task of tracking down Benny Peak, probably through every saloon in Piñon. He had to get that reata. So far Jesse Lester didn't know about Burke's mission in the Rio Desperado country. If Benny got that rope back to him and told him where he had found it . . .

Burke finished his beer and waved a refusal for a refill. "Be back later," he said. He eyed Garvey. "I'm refitting out," he added. "Got me a new slicker. Now that I got a job with the Double Bar H, I can afford to get a new outfit. Need a few other things. New bridle and bit. Cartridges. Stetson. Yeh, and a new rope."

"You won't have any trouble getting them in Piñon," said Garvey.

"I usually fancy a rawhide rope," said Burke. "Hard to get a good one these days. Have to settle for a grass rope I guess."

One of the men at the bar turned. "Benny Peak was in here awhile back, packing a goodlooking rawhide rope. Four stranded. *Bueno*."

"Would he sell it?" asked Burke. "Maybe he needs it in his work though."

They all laughed. "Benny?" said the man. "Hell, that rope ain't no use to him other than to sell it and get money for more forty-rod."

"Where can I find him?" asked Burke.

The man shrugged. "I heard him say he thought Jesse Lester might be interested in that rope. Mebbe he went over to the Lester place. Right up this next street, Mister. White painted cottage, picket fence, and window boxes."

"Thanks," said Burke quickly. "I know Jesse. I worked with him today. Maybe I can talk him out of it." He left the saloon and walked up the side street toward the place where he and Jesse had killed Harv and Curly. He looked back over his shoulder as he neared the fire ruined house in which Curly had placed himself in ambush. He saw that the Lester house was unlighted. Just as he passed the gaping window of the burned building he heard a hollow groan. His heart skipped a beat. He looked toward the window and saw a head bobbing up, exactly as he had seen the head of Curly Carter. Instinct triggered Burke. He jumped to one side, clawed beneath his unbuttoned slicker and had his Colt out and cocked before he had time to think.

The head sank out of sight and then reappeared and Burke could see the raddled face of a one-eyed drunk He sheathed the sixgun and walked to the window. "What's wrong?" he asked.

The man hiccupped. "Come in here out'a the rain," he said. He shook his head. "Couldn't get out'a the damned window."

"You're Benny Peak, aren't you?"

"Yeh."

Burke looked up and down the street. "You had a rawhide reata for sale. What did you do with it?"

Benny hiccupped again. "Left it at Jesse Lester's place."

"Did you tell him where you found it?"

Benny tried to focus his eyes. "Eh?"

Burked handed him a five dollar bill. "Where did you find it?"

"Wrapped in a dirty ol' slicker, stuck in a ramada over on Front Street. Sold the slicker to that skinflint Max Green. Figgered Jesse Lester might want to buy that rope." Benny eyed Burke more closely. "Who're you?"

"Never mind. Was Jesse home?"

"No. Front door was unlocked. Left the rope there with a note for Jesse."

Burke gave him a hand out of the window and watched him stagger up toward the main street. He was drunk enough to black out that night, but for a time he might mouth off that he had met Burke and that Burke was interested in that mysterious reata. Burke would have to chance it. He walked quickly up the street, walked to the barn and stepped inside of it to eye the darkened house. He'd have to chance going in there after that damned rope. He walked softly to the house and kept close to the side of it as he moved to the front. The place was deserted. He stepped up onto the porch and padded to the front door. He tried the knob and the door swung open easily. Burke stepped inside and closed the door behind him. He risked lighting a match to look for the rope. There was no sign of it. He blew out the match. Had Benny been lying, or was he too drunk to remember where he had left the reata? Burke cursed under his breath. He worked all through the neat living room and there was no sign of the rope.

Burke opened the door that led into a hallway that ran the length of the house to the kitchen. Other doors opened onto it from each side. He opened the first door and stepped into a bedroom, obviously a man's room, and Jesse's of course. There were ropes in the room, one of them was braided rawhide, but was a six stranded rope, while the other rope was Manila.

He shook his head. Every minute he

stayed in that silent house seemed like half an hour. He walked softly into the hallway and toward the kitchen and just as he passed a door it swung open and someone stood there. Once again Burke's instincts reacted and he swung short and hard with a right, catching the unknown on the side of the head. It was the subtle fragrance of perfume, mingled with the ripe odor of whiskey reached his nostrils.

He looked down at the unconscious form of Belle Lester. Burke picked up the luscious body and carried it to the bed. He thanked God he had not marked her face. Quickly he scouted the remaining rooms of the tomes, to find them deserted, and with no sign of the rope he wanted so desperately.

Burke went back to the room. She lay as he had left her. He filled a basin with water and reached for a cloth with which to bathe her temples. He turned. She was awake and watching him. Her slim right hand held a double-barreled derringer. "Stay right where you are, Mister Dane," she said quietly.

He eyed the little gun with the big bite. "I wasn't thinking of moving," he said pleasantly.

"What are you looking for, Mister Dane?"

"What makes you think I was looking for something?" he asked.

"Why else would you be prowling about a darkened house?"

Burke tilted his head to one side. "I knew Jesse wasn't around," he said quietly.

"And"

"I thought you might be home."

"So, when you *do* see me, you knock me out."

"You startled me, Miss Belle."

She shook her head a little. It was then that Burke noticed the partly empty bottle on the night stand beside the bed. Miss Belle had a bellyful. She was on a high lonesome in the darkened house. She just might be drunk enough for him to play out his game of bluff. "I thought for a minute it was Clete Hinch," she said a little thickly.

"Does he make a practice of visiting you like this?"

She shook her head again. "Jesse would kill him if he found him in here with me, Mister Dane." She leaned her head forward. "Just as he'd kill you if he walked in here now."

"Protecting his sister's beauty and virtue."

She stared at him and then she laughed. "Virtue? What virtue?"

"Can I put down this basin?"

"Go on."

She laughed again as he placed the basin on the dresser and turned to look at her. "The mysterious Man from New Mexico gets trapped in a lady's boudoir like a kid stealing apples," she said.

Burke grinned a little. It was rather amusing. It might turn out to be far from amusing if Clete Hinch or Jesse Lester walked in.

"Pour me a drink," she said.

He didn't argue. She just might get drunk enough to pass out. He knew now he hadn't really hit her hard enough to knock her out. The whiskey had helped the blow along. He poured her a drink. "Help yourself," she said.

He poured himself a drink and handed the other one to her. She took it in her left hand and downed it quickly. She shook her head as the hard stuff hit her stomach. Burke leaned against the wall. The window near him was partly open and he might have to leave in a hurry.

"You *were* looking for something, Mister Dane," she said in a low voice.

He sat down on the edge of the bed and her body moved toward him because of the slope of the mattress. She put down her gun hand to steady herself and a big hard hand closed on her wrist, pinning it to the spread. "Let go of it," he said. She tried to pull her hand free but the pressure of his grip numbed it. She released the derringer. Burke emptied it and placed it on the night stand.

"What are you going to do now?" she said. Her mouth was partly open and her breath came quickly.

"Get out of here," he said.

"No you won't, Mister Dane. You'll stay here as long as I want you to."

"Why?"

"Don't you know?"

He stared at her, half believing her implication, remembering the almost haughty look she had given him when she had first met him. She was quite different now from the well dressed young woman he remembered. He likened her now to other women he had known in the plushier bordellos of the West.

"Jesse won't be back for hours," she said. "He's with Sally Depree."

"Figures."

She laughed softly. "So, he's with a shady lady, and his sister is playing the same game with a man he thinks is his friend. The man to whom he owes his life."

He stared at her again. She drew herself close to him. She kissed him and Burke pulled away from her. The temptation was almost overpowering but the situation was too dangerous, and the danger drove all thoughts of dalliance from his mind. "What's your game, Belle?" he asked.

She stared uncomprehendingly at him. "Well?" he said.

Her open hand caught him stingingly across the mouth and drew blood. She clawed at his face with her long nailed fingers until he caught her slim wrists and gripped them tightly. He moved his face close to hers. "Listen, Belle," he said harshly. "I'm not fool enough to be playing games with Jesse Lester's beloved sister as long as he's walking around with two Colts hanging at his thighs, nor do I want Clete Hinch to find out I'm in his lady friend's bedroom in the dark. What's your game, Belle?"

She bowed her head a little. "Let me go, Burke," she said quietly.

He released her. He walked to the door and peered into the dark hallway.

"Always the cautious one, aren't you?" she said.

"It keeps me alive, Belle," he said dryly.

"It isn't a trap for you, Burke. If Jesse

166

or Clete knew you were in here, they'd kill you without thinking twice about it."

"The rope you are looking for is under the bed," she said.

For a moment he was startled. He downed his drink.

"It's Jesse's rope all right. Benny Peak found it wrapped in your slicker, Burke."

"He said he left it here with a note."

"I told him to tell you that if you asked him."

"Why?"

"I wanted to talk to you."

Burke stared at her. "But why?"

"You didn't fool me, Burke. You came to the Rio Desperado country for a reason, and it wasn't to work for Ben Hinch. You're a gunfighter, but not of the same stamp as the men of the Double Bar H. You had me fooled for awhile. I know who and what you are, Burke Dane."

A cold feeling fled through his body. "Go on."

"You're Burke Dane, sure enough. But what no one else around here knows, but myself and one other person is that you're Charley Mayo's half brother."

In the silence that followed Burke thought of how easy it would be to clamp those big, hard hands of his about that alabaster neck and squeeze the life out of the lovely young woman so close to him.

"Don't worry," she said at last. "I'm not going to talk."

"Who else knows?"

She laughed shortly. "You'd never know. I'll tell you though. It's Sally Depree. She saw you once or twice in Albuquerque a year or so ago."

Then Burke remembered his first meeting with Sally Depree. "Burke Dane," she had said. "I'm almost tempted to ask if that is your real name, Mister Dane. It sounds almost familiar."

"Seems as though Sally is mad about my brother. . . She might not act like it, but Jesse means everything to her. She also knows I'd fight tooth and nail to keep Jesse from marrying her."

"Not in your social strata, is that it, Belle?" asked Burke dryly.

Belle flushed. "Well said, Mister Dane. My brother means a great deal to me. More than he does to Sally Depree, or anyone else. That was why I meant to marry Clete Hinch. It would only be a matter of time before Jesse would be killed by them. Clete hates his guts, but lets him alone because of me. Ben Hinch wouldn't let anything happen to his future daughter-in-law's beloved brother. When Ben is gone, I, as Clete's wife, could help make a future for Jesse."

"Beside Clete throughout eternity, Belle?" asked Burke softly.

She reached for the bottle and drank deeply. She took a deep breath. "I hate his guts," she said bitterly.

"You'd sacrifice your whole life and happiness to make sure Jesse had a future?"

"It wasn't until you came here looking for the men who had lynched your brother that I realized how wrong I was. But there is a solution, Burke."

"Go on," he said. His eyes narrowed.

She eyed him closely. "Jesse likes you.

He'd do anything for you. He'd listen to you, Burke."

"Him?" Burke laughed harshly. "That lobo of a kid wouldn't listen to Jesus Christ himself!"

"You're wrong! I know."

"So what is the solution?"

She gripped his arm. "If I help you get back the money that was taken from your brother, will you take Jessie and me with you?"

He stared at her. "Just exactly what do you mean?"

She drew closer to him and held her face up to his. "Take us with you, Burke! There's no way other than that where we can escape Clete Hinch. He'd kill both Jesse and me without a thought if we ran out on him. Up until the time you came here, I thought we were doomed, but now I know that if anyone can help us, it's you."

The rain suddenly beat a tattoo against the side of the house. Burke wet his lips and looked at the beauty so close to him.

"You haven't told me everything," he said.

"Take us with you, Burke, after I help you get the money. When we are free from this damned place, marry me. Jesse will listen to you if I am your wife. I'll make a good wife to you, Burke. Please, Burke!"

He stood up. "There is such a thing as love, Belle," he said softly.

"For such a man as *you?* A born killer?" she laughed. "Tell me anything but that, Burke. When have you ever experienced love?"

He half closed his eyes and the lovely face of Marion Mayo came swiftly across the rain swept mountains to haunt him, as it had for so many years when loneliness was his constant riding companion.

"Burke?" she said questioningly.

He poured a drink and downed it, but alcohol seemed to have no effect on him that night.

"Burke?"

He turned. "All right," he said. "It's a deal."

She got up on her knees on the rumpled bed and held out her arms. He drew her close and kissed her, passing his hands up and down the back of her head and the small of her back. She drew back. "Stay with me a little while," she said pleadingly.

"No time, Belle," he said quickly. "That will come later, I assure you."

There was a hurt look on her flushed face. She reached for the bottle, but he intercepted her. "Get dressed," he said. "I want you to show me where the money is."

"And Clete Hinch?" she said.

"Yes."

He stepped back as she got out of the bed. "Who killed my brother, Belle?" he asked.

"Clete led the party that followed him. He had Curly Carter, Joe Moss, Harv Clayton and Larry Newman with him."

"And Jesse?"

"No," she said quickly. "It was Clete that borrowed Jesse's rope."

"Don't lie to me, Belle!"

She came to him and kissed him. "I'm not lying, Burke," she said, and he knew in his heart that she was not. He walked to the door and closed it behind him to let her get dressed, and as he walked to the living room he drew his sleeve quickly across his mouth to wipe away the taste of her kisses.

9

THE fine rain was slanting down upon Piñon and the dark skies were silver threaded now and then by the faint flashing of the lightning. The river was rising and the subdued roaring played an undertone to the sound of the rain and the sweeping wind that came down from Windy Pass. Burke Dane halted at the top of the covered outside stairs in the rear of the big rambling hotel. Belle Lester pressed up close behind him. "Clete's suite is just beyond the main staircase, Burke," she whispered.

Burke nodded. "Do you think he's there?"

"Yes."

"How do you know?"

"What time is it?"

He looked at her over his shoulder. "A little after nine o'clock. Why?"

She smiled faintly. "He's expecting me."

"That's why you insisted on dressing up?"

"You've got the general idea, Mister Dane."

Burke eased open the door and peered into the dimly lighted hallway. There was no sign of life. He peeled off his slicker and hung it over the railing. "You're sure the money is in his suite?" he asked.

"It was, last time I was in it."

"You *do* get around, don't you, Belle?" Burke eased his Colt in its sheath. "Why doesn't he keep it in the bank?"

She laughed. "Because he was playing with money that belonged to his father. Ben Hinch allows his beloved son a free rein in almost anything, but he doesn't allow Clete to play with Hinch money. When Charley Mayo beat Clete at poker, he was signing his own death warrant. Clete asked Charley Mayo not to mention to Ben Hinch that he had won heavily from Clete. Mayo bought his cattle from Ben and started back to New Mexico with the cattle and the remainder of his winnings. He never got there, as you well know."

Burke turned to look at her. "Who rode with him, Belle?"

"I've already told you, Burke."

"When?" Burke eyed her closely. "You said Clete led the party that followed him. Clete, Curly Carter, Joe Moss, Harv Clayton and Larry Newman."

"It wasn't exactly like that, Burke. Mayo hired, or *thought* he had hired, Carter, Moss and Clayton. They rode with him from the valley, followed by Clete and Larry. I don't have to fill in any details now, do I?"

Burke closed his eyes, sickened by Clete's duplicity and murderous mind. Poor Charley had never had the suspicious mind that had saved Burke's life more than once.

"Clete is just waiting for a chance to get that money back where it belongs without his father finding out what had happened. God help Clete if his father ever does find out."

"God help Clete anyway," said Burke softly. He started forward, but she drew him back and shook her head. "What's wrong?" he asked.

"He's expecting me, Burke. Let me go ahead. I promise to keep his mind occupied until you get there."

"I hate hiding behind a woman's skirts, Belle."

She passed him, patted his cheek, then kissed him lightly. "Even mine, Burke?" She swished gracefully down the wide carpeted hallway.

Burke shook his head in admiration. There was a lot of Jesse in Belle, and maybe—in the long run—Belle was the more to be admired for certain qualities. He watched her tap on the door of Clete's suite, then enter, closing the door behind her. Burke gave her five minutes, then padded softly down the long hallway. Somewhere on the same floor was Sally Depree's room. Belle had insisted that they get Jesse when they were through with Clete. She had a lot more confidence in that thought than did Burke.

Personally Burke was ready to leave after he had the money and the scalp of Clete Hinch.

He stepped into a linen closet just across the hall from Clete's room. He didn't like this business of being indoors, especially being on the second floor, but there was no helping it. Minutes ticked past and the tension grew until at last Burke knew he had to make his move.

He drew his Colt, walked quickly across the hallway, gripped the knob and turned it easily. The door swung open. He stepped into a brightly lighted room. Clete Hinch sat at the far side of a marble-topped table, with Belle, in all her glory, sat on a chaise lounge near the draped window. For a second Burke knew he should run, then he heard the door close just behind him. Something hard pressed into the small of his back.

"Stand easy, *Mister* Dane," said a familiar voice. It was that of Larry Newman.

Burke looked at Belle. She had betrayed him!

Clete slowly raised his right hand and rested it on the table. A nickel-plated Colt was aimed right at Burke's belly. Something moved at the right of the big room and a man stepped out from behind a drapery with a Winchester in his hands. Burke recognized him as the man named Shorty, from the Double Bar H. Then another man came into the sitting room from the bedroom, holding a cocked Colt in his hand.

"Drop that sixshooter, Mister Dane," said Clete easily.

The Colt thudded on the carpeted floor and Burke raised his hands level with his face.

Clete smiled thinly. "The 'Man from New Mexico,' eh? Who did you think you were dealing with, Dane? Rank amateurs? This is the Rio Desperado country! Not the backwoods of New Mexico!"

"You hold all the aces," said Burke quietly. "Stop the heroics, *Mister* Hinch. Get on with the killing."

"Who did you think you were fooling,

Dane? We got a line on you within twenty-four hours after you arrived here."

Who had talked? The only person in Piñon who had even hinted at knowing Burke had been Sally Depree. It must have been her. Perhaps she had talked to Jesse Lester; perhaps Jesse, with his babyface and frankness only a thin disguise for his duplicity, had conspired with his sister to get Burke into the net with as little trouble as possible. If so, they did a neat job, and there would be but one answer to the question as far as Burke was concerned.

Print Campbell was sure that Burke Dane would never get back to the Valley of the Big Bonito. But he had to! Marion and her little ones depended on Burke. He'd have to cast the dice in a last wild throw—win or lose—take the stakes, or end up in a pine suit with brass handles for trimming, as Jesse Lester once suggested.

Clete smiled again. "Well, we've got plenty of rope here in the Valley, Mister Dane. A nice one for you, or anyone else who comes around here looking for trouble."

"How are you going to explain *this* murder to your old man?" asked Burke easily.

Clete's eyes narrowed. "What the hell do you mean?"

"It's a cinch he wasn't responsible for the death of my brother, Hinch. So happens your *father* hired me. Is he letting you take over the Double Bar H right under his nose? That isn't like Ben Hinch, Clete."

"He's suspicious of you!" snapped Clete.

"Maybe," agreed Burke. He smiled. "Well, go ahead, Clete, string me up, then explain it to your father. Damned if I wouldn't crawl out of my grave to listen to you explaining it too!"

"He might be right, Mister Hinch," said Larry Newman.

"You crawling out of this, Larry?" sneered Clete.

"You know better than that. I got no

use for this *hombre*, but I don't want to get into trouble with Ben Hinch."

"I'm running this show!" yelled Clete.

"Sure you are," soothed Burke. "You tell the boys that, Cletie."

"Damn you!" Clete jumped to his feet, and as he did so, a silent message sped from Belle Lester's lovely eyes to Burke Dane. The young woman jumped to her feet and snatched a heavy cutglass decanter from a side table. She swung it against the side of Clete's head and he went down heavily.

Belle grabbed Clete's gun from the table and fired at Shorty. The little man went down without a sound. Burke whirled, clamping a hand down on Newman's gunwrist. His Colt exploded, driving a slug into the floor. Burke's right fist smashed against Newman's jaw, driving him back against the door which flew open, letting Newman fall into the hallway. Burke whirled and drew his derringer, firing almost from floor level up at the man standing in the bedroom door. He grunted and staggered back and the second slug caught him full in the belly.

Belle darted across the room, raised a picture on the wall, and revealed a wall safe. "Keep guard!" she snapped at Burke. Burke picked up his Colt and then reloaded his derringer. Powder smoke was thick in the room. Burke picked up Shorty's Winchester from the man's stiffening hands. He walked to the door and kicked it open, Winchester at hip level, but there was no sign of Larry Newman in the hallway.

The safe clicked open. Belle took out a thick envelope and handed it to Burke. He flipped it open with a thumb, and saw the thick wad of bills in it. Belle picked up a Colt. "Let's get out of here," she said.

Burke looked at Clete. "I'm not done yet."

Her Colt prodded into his hard belly. "Forget him!" she snapped. "We're going to get Jesse and get out of this valley before dawn."

"I had two reasons for coming here," he said stubbornly.

"You kill Clete, and Ben Hinch will never stop hunting you down! Killing Clete won't bring back Charley Mayo, Burke! The money is yours. Now you keep your deal with me!" The Colt hammer clicked back under her thumb.

"All right," he said. She was using her head better than he was. He led the way along the hall, watching for a sudden movement. He remembered again Newman's threat, "I won't forget you, Dane. Ever."

Belle stopped at a door. She tried it and found it locked. She tapped on it. "Jesse? Sally?"

There was a soft rustling sound from within, then the door swung open. Sally Depree stood there, clad in a sheer negligee that did nothing to conceal, but instead accentuated her nakedness beneath it. The lamplight shone on her soft white skin, and on the little locket between her thrusting breasts. "Jesse ain't here," she said quickly. She paled at the look on Burke's face. He thrust her aside. Belle closed the door behind her. Jesse lay face downward on the bed, one slim hand resting on the floor, holding an empty whiskey glass in it.

Burke walked to the Kid and pulled him up from the bed. He shook the lolling figure and slapped the flushed face. "No use, Belle," he said over his shoulder. "He can't walk."

"Carry him, then," she said sharply.

"Leave him be!" cried Sally.

Belle looked coldly at her. "We're getting Jesse out of this hellhole of a valley," she said thinly, "and no one is going to stop us, Sally."

The girl laughed. "You're not out of it yet. How many men have you killed tonight, Burke Dane? How many more will you kill before they kill you!"

There was only one thing to do. "Sally," said Burke. As she looked at him he struck her neatly on her smooth, small jaw. He caught her before she hit the floor. It was only a matter of minutes to bind her with her sheer silk stockings and thrust a gag into her pretty little red lipped mouth. The last thing Burke did was to take the locket from her neck, wipe it hurriedly on his shirt, then thrust it into a pocket.

Belle carried the Winchester and led the way as Burke carried the Kid along the deserted hallway to the rear stairs. She snatched up Burke's slicker and hung it over the Kid as Burke carried him down the stairs.

Burke splashed through the muddy water of the alleyway, thinking incongruously of Belle Lester's fine satin slippers as she waded along behind him, cursing softly under her breath. There was so little time. Larry Newman wasn't sitting on his duff at that moment. He was up to no good, and it was only a matter of time before Clete Hinch came back to the world of the living and made an attempt to peddle a little more death before that wet night was over.

They reached the livery stable in safety. The three horses were saddled before Burke and Belle went to the hotel and the liveryman, with twenty bucks in his jeans, had vanished for the night. Belle hurriedly stripped off her finery in the dark and dressed herself in trail clothing. Burke hoisted the Kid into a saddle and lashed him there. They had need of his fast gun that night, but in his condition he could hardly see and think well enough to draw and shoot.

Burke led his horse and the Kid's out into the alley. Belle slid the door shut behind her horse. Burke looked at her. She smiled. "So far so good," she said.

"Yeh," he said dryly. He wished to God he was alone, but if it hadn't been for Belle Lester he'd be dead by now. A deal was a deal.

The rain slashed down as they reached the next street. Burke scouted ahead, then waved Belle on. She hurriedly crossed the street, and just as she did so, five horsemen splashed through the mud of the main street. Burke saw Larry Newman wave to them from the far side of the street.

Burke led the way along the alley until

they reached the next side street. He motioned to Belle to stay there. He took his Winchester and padded up to the main street, stepping into a deep doorway where he could see the wet bulk of the Hinch Hotel. Horses stood in the side street, and even as he watched he saw Larry Newman come out of the side entrance, helping Clete Hinch to a horse.

Burke hurried back to Belle. "Newman's gotten some help. Clete just joined them. They have horses. They'll cover the roads out of town. We've got to get to the bridge before they do!"

They mounted and rode to the east toward the roaring river, then turned up the street that paralleled the river. "Take him across," said Burke. Belle led the Kid's horse across the bridge. A man shouted down the street.

Burke stepped out from behind the corner building and placed a shot in the leading horse. The man went down with a grunt into the cold mud. It wasn't either Hinch or Newman. Burke spurred the dun across the bridge. Water was already lapping over the upstream side. By dawn the bridge would either be swept away or feet deep in flood water. The icy thought came to him that they must again cross the river before hitting the road to Windy Pass. There was no other way as close as that to escape the Valley of the Rio Desperado. The bridge spanning the East Fork, miles to the east, was a structure long past its prime. If it was washed away before they crossed, they would be trapped.

On the far side of the river Burke turned and churned out half a dozen slugs down the center of the bridge, then he turned and galloped off after Belle and the Kid.

Time and time again in the next hours he waited as Belle went on through the wet darkness with Jesse, hoping their pursuers had given up. But twice more he had to fire back at them, and he knew then that Clete Hinch could never let Burke escape that damned valley with the money that rightfully belonged to Marion Mayo. If Burke didn't feel responsible for

Belle and the Kid he would have been able to make it, he was quite sure of that.

Lightning crackled now and again across the streaming skies as they rode steadily toward the crossing of the East Fork. An hour before dawn Jesse Lester managed to get enough sense back into his drugged head to sit up in the saddle, and also enough sense to keep his mouth shut when he saw the taut faces of his sister and Burke Dane. Jesse knew well enough what would happen to all of them if Clete Hinch caught up with them.

They could hear the roaring of the East Fork long before they reached it, and when they did, a flood of sickness welled up within them, for the water was running inches deep across the floor of the bridge, and the structure was actually curved from the great pressure of the rising flood waters.

"The weight of a horse will cave in that damned thing," said Jesse thickly.

"We can't swim them across," said Burke.

"We can't go back," said Belle flatly.

Burke spat into the flood, then dismounted. He took the reins and started out on the sagging bridge, feeling the pull and tug of the flood. The water was at boot top level, and cold as ice. His heart was in his throat as he moved across foot by foot. It took him fifteen minutes to cross and even as he reached the safety of the ground something snapped in the middle of the bridge and it assumed a sharper curve.

The Kid was next. The mid-bridge water was rushing about his knees and even as he worked his way closer to the bank it rose above them. He led his horse up the bank. There was a sickly white look on his face. "She can't make it, Burke," he said. "Let her go back. They won't kill a woman. She's got Clete wrapped around her little finger."

"Not now," said Burke quietly. "That bastard won't ever forgive her for what she did."

The young woman led her mare to the end of the bridge and looked across at them. Burke's heart went out to her. He should have let her come across first, but if the bridge had failed them then, she would have been surely lost. Belle started across, with the water swirling about her thighs.

"Sheer guts," said Jesse. "That's my *sister*, Burke!"

"Shut up!" snapped Burke. He reached for his reata and coiled it in his left hand, letting the loop hang loosely at his side. "Get your rope, Kid."

She was twenty feet from the bank when the shot rang out from the west bank and the mare whinnied in pain, tearing loose the reins from Belle's hands. The mare floundered about and stepped from the side of the bridge. In an instant the surging waters carried her swiftly downstream and out of sight.

Burke threw his loop neatly about Belle's shoulders. She had the presence of mind to thrust her arms through the loop and settle the reata under her armpits. Burke began to pull her toward the bank, hand over hand.

Orange-red blossoms of gunfire dotted

the darkness on the far bank. Hungry lead whined through the air. Slugs spurted the racing waters.

"Shoot, damn you!" yelled Burke to the Kid.

Jesse drew his Colts and began to pour hot lead across the river. Just as Belle reached the bank and Burke got his arms about her he felt her jerk. "Are you hit?" he asked.

"Just a skinning, Burke," she cried.

"Can we hold 'em here at the river?" said Jesse as he reloaded.

Burke looked closely at the young woman. She was holding her full lower lip between her white teeth. "Let's pull leather," he said. He hoisted Belle up into his saddle and led the dun along the muddy road. Jesse fired his guns dry, then followed them. Burke looked back at the bend in the road. Already one of them was halfway across the bridge and another of them had started across. Maybe the Kid had been right. Burke looked up at Belle. Her face was white and set. There was no time to examine her wound.

The sky was graying and the rain was slackening when they reached the foot of Windy Pass. An acute weariness flowed through Burke as he slogged on.

"Maybe we'd better make a stand, Burke?" said the Kid.

"Keep moving, damn you!" roared Burke.

Even as he spoke a gun cracked flatly, from *ahead* of them, and the Kid's horse went down thrashing. Burked jumped to one side and hauled on the reins of the dun. He led it into the thick wetbrush and yanked his Winchester free from its scabbard. Then a rifle flashed behind them, followed by the reports of several others. A slug whipped through the top of Burke's soaked Stetson.

"Trapped, by God!" snarled the Kid. "We should'a held 'em at the bridge!"

Then it was quiet as the sky lightened and the powdersmoke drifted off on the freshening wind.

"How many of them?" asked the Kid softly.

"Six, counting Hinch and Newman."

"Great."

Burke checked the Winchester, then peeled off his slicker and tossed his hat to one side. "Stay here," he said. "I'll try a little bushwhacking."

"Let me go!"

Burke looked at him. "In *your* condition? You wouldn't have a chance, Kid." He vanished into the wet and clinging brush.

Jesse held his cocked Colts in each hand. He wet his dry lips. His head pounded like a tom-tom and the dregs of his liquor-drinking were playing hell with his guts. He shook his head. Belle opened her eyes. She winced a little as she moved. The Winchester was leaning against a log. She gripped it, steadied herself, then brought it down hard on her brother's head. Jesse sank to the soaked ground and lay still. A thin trickle of blood traced a zigzag course down the side of his white face.

10

THE icy water soaked through Burke's clothing as he bellied through the brush. He crawled across a ditch that was six inches deep in running water and lay flat against the ground, trying to skylight some of their pursuers. It beat him as to how some of them had gotten ahead of them on that road, but the fact that Burke was afoot and that Belle had been in greater pain than she had let on, had slowed them too much to reach the top of the pass before Hinch and his corrida did.

Burke cocked the Winchester. He saw a vague movement in the brush on the far side of the road. He picked up a rock and heaved it high overhead to land behind whoever was over there. A sudden movement betrayed the man. Burke got to his knees and fired twice and the lead found its mark. The man went down silently.

Burke dropped flat and rolled over and over in the icy mud as bullets pocked the place from where he had fired. One down, five to go. Damn that drunken Kid anyway! He had left it all up to Burke, and the odds were far too high against one man.

Burke lay still, peering through the dripping brush as the light grew steadily. Ragged dark clouds raced across the cold gray sky. The road was empty of life. It was too quiet to suit Burke. He bellied along the ditch, rounding a huge boulder and as he peered across the road he saw a man running across it. He fired three times and the man went spinning down the wet slope, screaming like a stuck pig.

Smoke rifted as the wind shifted a little. There were still four of them in those wet woods waiting for a shot at Burke. What the hell was the Kid doing? Burke lay flat and waited. There was nothing else he could do. They'd have to reveal themselves to him, for if they saw him, the odds were that at least one of them would get in a disabling or killing shot.

Burke moved a little. A gun snapped and the slug smashed into the rick inches from his face, stinging it with lead fragments. He winced in pain and raised his body. As he did so a gun cracked again and the slug smashed into his left boot heel, ripping it cleanly off and numbing his left foot. He scuttled for cover. As he did, he saw a movement in the brush. He snapped up the rifle and fired. The gun jerked in his hands. It didn't sound right. He peered along the wet barrel and saw a bulge on it, terminating in a split. He cursed under his breath. He had accidentally plugged the barrel with mud and the gas and slug of the cartridge he fired ruined the barrel.

He drew his Colt and checked it. He was at a distinct disadvantage now. One pistolman against four riflemen, and they were Double Bar H riflemen—three of them paid gunfighters. They wouldn't miss.

Suddenly there was an outburst of rifle

firing from the place where Belle and the Kid lay hidden. A man yelled in savage pain. Another darted out of the brush, falling to his knees to claw at his shoulder. A slug drove him face flat into the mud and he lay still. Burke jumped to his feet and rounded the boulder. A gun cracked and the slug deeply skinned his left shoulder and the pain of it drove him staggering out into the open road before he could help it. He dropped his Colt and clawed for it.

"Leave it be!" said the flat, cold voice.

Burke looked up into the set face of Larry Newman, Colt in hand. Burke came up at an angle, driving in hard at the gunfighter as the Colt exploded, ripping through Burke's jacket. Burke brought a knee up into Newman's groin and as the gunfighter grunted in agony, Burke tried to rip his gun away from him. The sixshooter slammed out a shot and the lead traced a burning course up Burke's left forearm to lodge in the hard muscle above the elbow joint. Before he fell he ripped out his derringer and fired it upward into Newman's chin two feet away, and the man's face seemed to explode as the soft-nosed slug drove home to his brain.

Sheer and excruciating pain flowed through Burke Dane and he knew he was through fighting. He fell flat on his face and managed to cock the derringer for the last cartridge in it. It was then he saw Clete Hinch running up the road toward him with Winchester in hand. There was a look of complete triumph on the man's face, mingled with the sheer lust of killing. He came on, passing the place where Belle and the Kid were hidden, and Burke Dane knew that death, in the shape of Clete Hinch, was on its swift and merciless way to him.

"Clete! Clete Hinch!" cried the voice.

The man turned. Belle Lester stepped out into the road, Winchester at hip level, face set and taut, with lines etched deeply on the beauty of it. Even as he stared she fired from the hip, reloaded and fired again. Hinch went down, and three more slugs rapped into his prone body. His hands dug into the cold mud then stiffened. A moment later Belle Lester fell beside him.

Burke forced himself to his feet. The woods were quiet again. He knew that none of them were left alive. He bound his wound with his scarf and walked to Belle. He turned her over and looked into her sightless eyes.

The Kid was sitting up, holding his battered head in his hands. "I never saw her buffalo me, Burke," he said.

Burke dropped on the log and passed out completely. When he came to, he found that the Kid had neatly bandaged his wound.

"The slug went clean through," said Jesse. "Damned lucky for you it didn't hit the bone."

They wrapped Belle's body in a blanket and placed it on one of the horses the Double Bar H men would never need again. The Kid found a mount and they led the horse carrying Belle's body up the long road toward the top of Windy Pass. They never looked back. After the slaughter of that morning, it was hardly likely Ben Hinch would attempt a pursuit. Besides, Ben Hinch knew better than to try his power beyond the Valley of the Rio Desperado.

At the top of the pass, Burke looked back, down on the swirling mists of the Valley of the Rio Desperado, as he did once before, not so long ago, wondering what was in store for him in that cold shroud of mist and rain. He did what he had set out to do, but at a terrible price. He knew now that his gunfighting days were over forever. The thought of Marion Mayo came to him from the eastern side of the windswept pass. If she'd have him, he'd settle down, but somehow he knew that a part of him was gone forever, and that it would be buried in the grave with the lovely body of Belle Lester.

"Come on, Kid," he said.

"Where to, Burke?"

"The Valley of the Big Bonito."

"What's there, *amigo?*"

Burke smiled evenly. "Your whole future life, Kid, if you want to make it that way. Once you descend the eastern side of Windy Pass, you can make your own decision."

As they started down toward the Valley of the Little Bonito the sun appeared through a rift in the hurrying clouds and shone down on the two horsemen.

Jesse Lester rolled a cigarette and handed it to Burke, then rolled one for himself. He lighted both cigarettes, blew out a puff of smoke and said quietly, "I owe it to Belle, Burke. I've made up my mind."

To Burke it seemed as though somehow in the tangled way of life and death, his younger brother had been returned to him in the form of Jesse Lester. There was no use in looking back. The future beckoned. It was better that way. Somewhere in the woods below the pass a jay scolded. A doe bounded cleanly across the road. The clouds drifted off and the drying sun shined fully on the Valley of the Little Bonito. The storm was over.

Other titles in the
Linford Western Library:

TOP HAND
by Wade Everett

The Broken T was big enough for a man on the run to hire out as a cowhand and be safe. But no ranch is big enough to let a man hide from himself.

GUN WOLVES OF LOBO BASIN
by Lee Floren

The Feud was a blood debt. When Smoke Talbot found the outlaws who gunned down his folks he aimed to nail their hide to the barn door.

SHOTGUN SHARKEY
by Marshall Grover

The westbound coach carrying the indomitable Larry and Stretch and their mixed bag of allies headed for a shooting showdown.

McALLISTER ON THE COMANCHE CROSSING
by Matt Chisholm

The Comanche, deadly warriors and the finest horsemen in the world, reckon McAllister owes them a life—and the trail is soaked with the blood of the men who had tried to outrun them before.

QUICK-TRIGGER COUNTRY
by Clem Colt

Turkey Red hooked up with Curly Bill Graham's outlaw crew and soon made a name for himself. But wholesale murder was out of Turk's line, so when range war flared he bucked the whole border gang alone . . .

PISTOL LAW
by Paul Evan Lehman

Lance Jones came back to Mustang for just one thing—Revenge! Revenge on the people who had him thrown in jail; on the crooked marshal; on the human vulture who had already taken over the town. Now it was Lance's turn . . .

GUNSLINGER'S RANGE
by Jackson Cole

Three escaped convicts are out for revenge. They won't rest until they put a bullet through the head of the dirty snake who locked them behind bars.

RUSTLER'S TRAIL
by Lee Floren

Jim Carlin knew he would have to stand up and fight because he had staked his claim right in the middle of Big Ike Outland's best grass. Jim also had a score to settle with his renegade brother.

Larry and Stretch:
THE TRUTH ABOUT SNAKE RIDGE
by Marshall Grover

The troubleshooters came to San Cristobal to help the needy. For Larry and Stretch the turmoil began with a brawl, then an ambush, and then another attempt on their lives—all in one day.

WOLF DOG RANGE
by Lee Floren

Montana was big country, but not big enough for a ruthless land-grabber like Will Ardery. He would stop at nothing, unless something stopped him first—like a bullet from Pete Manly's gun.

Larry and Stretch: DEVIL'S DINERO
by Marshall Grover

Plagued by remorse, a rich old reprobate hired the Texas Troubleshooters to deliver a fortune in greenbacks to each of his victims. Even before Larry and Stretch rode out of Cheyenne, a traitor was selling the secret and the hunt was on.

CAMPAIGNING
by Jim Miller

Ambushed on the Santa Fe trail, Sean Callahan is saved from dying by two Indian strangers. Then the trio is joined by a former slave called Hannibal. But there'll be more lead and arrows flying before the band join the legendary Kit Carson in his campaign against the Comanches.

DONOVAN
by Elmer Kelton

Donovan was supposed to be dead. The town had buried him years before when Uncle Joe Vickers had fired off both barrels of a shotgun into the vicious outlaw's face as he was escaping from jail. Now Uncle Joe had been shot—in just the same way.

CODE OF THE GUN
by Gordon D. Shirreffs

MacLean came riding home with saddle-tramp written all over him, but sewn in his shirt-lining was an Arizona Ranger's star. MacLean had his own personal score to settle—in blood and violence!

GAMBLER'S GUN LUCK
by Brett Austen

Gamblers hands are clean and quick with cards, guns and women. But their names are black, and they seldom live long. Parker was a hell of a gambler. It was his life—or his death . . .

ORPHAN'S PREFERRED
by Jim Miller

A boy in a hurry to be a man, Sean Callahan answers the call of the Pony Express. With a little help from his Uncle Jim and the Navy Colt .36, Sean fights Indians and outlaws to get the mail through.

DAY OF THE BUZZARD
by T. V. Olsen

All Val Penmark cared about was getting the men who killed his wife. All young Jason Drum cared about was getting back his family's life savings. He could not understand the ruthless kind of hate Penmark nursed in his guts.

THE MANHUNTER
by Gordon D. Shirreffs

Lee Kershaw knew that every Rurale in the territory was on the lookout for him. But the offer of $5,000 in gold to find five small pieces of leather was too good to turn down.

RIFLES ON THE RANGE
by Lee Floren

Doc Mike and the farmer stood there alone between Smith and Watson. Doc Mike knew what was coming. There was this moment of stillness, a clock-tick of eternity, and then the roar would start. And somebody would die . . .

HARTIGAN
by Marshall Grover

Hartigan had come to Cornerstone to die. He chose the time and the place, but he did not fight alone. Side by side with Nevada Jim, the territory's unofficial protector, they challenged the killers—and Main Street became a battlefield.

HARSH RECKONING
by Phil Ketchum

The minute Brand showed up at his ranch after being illegally jailed, people started shooting at him. But five years of keeping himself alive in a brutal prison had made him tough and careless about who he gunned down . . .

FIGHTING RAMROD
by Charles N. Heckelmann

Most men would have cut their losses, but Frazer counted the bullets in his guns and said he'd soak the range in blood before he'd give up another inch of what was his.

LONE GUN
by Eric Allen

Smoke Blackbird had been away too long. The Lequires had seized the Blackbird farm, forcing the Indians and settlers off, and no one seemed willing to fight! He had to fight alone.

THE THIRD RIDER
by Barry Cord

Mel Rawlins wasn't going to let anything stand in his way. His father was murdered, his two brothers gone. Now Mel rode for vengeance.

RIDE A LONE TRAIL
by Gordon D. Shirreffs

The valley was about to explode into open range war. All it needed was the fuse and Ken Macklin was it.

ARIZONA DRIFTERS
by W. C. Tuttle

When drifting Dutton and Lonnie Steelman decide to become partners they find that they have a common enemy in the formidable Thurston brothers.

TOMBSTONE
by Matt Braun

Wells Fargo paid Luke Starbuck to outgun the silver-thieving stagecoach gang at Tombstone. Before long Luke can see the only thing bearing fruit in this eldorado will be the gallows tree.

HIGH BORDER RIDERS
by Lee Floren

Buckshot McKee and Tortilla Joe cut the trail of a border tough who was running Mexican beef into Texas. They stopped the smuggler in his tracks.

HARD MAN WITH A GUN
by Charles N. Heckelmann

After Bob Keegan lost the girl he loved and the ranch he had sweated blood to build, he had nothing left but his guts and his guns but he figured that was enough.

BRETT RANDALL, GAMBLER
by E. B. Mann

Larry Day had the choice of running away from the law or of assuming a dead man's place. No matter what he decided he was bound to end up dead.

THE GUNSHARP
by William R. Cox

The Eggerleys weren't very smart. They trained their sights on Will Carney and Arizona's biggest blood bath began.

THE DEPUTY OF SAN RIANO
by Lawrence A. Keating and
Al. P. Nelson

When a man fell dead from his horse, Ed Grant was spotted riding away from the scene. The deputy sheriff rode out after him and came up against everything from gunfire to dynamite.

SUNDANCE: IRON MEN
by Peter McCurtin

Sundance, assigned to save the railroad from a murder spree, soon came to realise that he'd have to fight fire with fire, bullets with bullets and death with death!

FARGO: MASSACRE RIVER
by John Benteen

Fargo spurred his horse to the edge of the road. The ambushers up ahead had now blocked the road. Fargo's convoy was a jumble, a perfect target for the insurgents' weapons!

SUNDANCE:
DEATH IN THE LAVA
by John Benteen

The land echoed with the thundering hoofs of Modoc ponies. In minutes they swooped down and captured the wagon train and its cargo of gold. But now the halfbreed they called Sundance was going after it, and he swore nothing would stand in his way.

GUNS OF FURY
by Ernest Haycox

Dane Starr, alias Dan Smith, wanted to close the door on his past and hang up his guns, but people wouldn't let him. Good men wanted him to settle their scores for them. Bad men thought they were faster and itched to prove it. Starr had to keep killing just to stay alive.

FARGO: PANAMA GOLD
by John Benteen

Cleve Buckner was recruiting an army of killers, gunmen and deserters from all over Central America. With foreign money behind him, Buckner was going to destroy the Panama Canal before it could be completed. Fargo's job was to stop Buckner—and to eliminate him once and for all!

FARGO: THE SHARPSHOOTERS
by John Benteen

The Canfield clan, thirty strong, were raising hell in Texas. One of them had shot a Texas Ranger, and the Rangers had to bring in the killer. Fargo was tough enough to hold his own against the whole clan.

SUNDANCE: OVERKILL
by John Benteen

Sundance's reputation as a fighting man had spread. There was no job too tough for the halfbreed to handle. So when a wealthy banker's daughter was kidnapped by the Cheyenne, he offered Sundance $10,000 to rescue the girl.

HELL RIDERS
by Steve Mensing

Wade Walker's kid brother, Duane, was locked up in the Silver City jail facing a rope at dawn. Wade was a ruthless outlaw, but he was smart, and he had vowed to have his brother out of jail before morning!

DESERT OF THE DAMNED
by Nelson Nye

The law was after him for the murder of a marshal—a murder he didn't commit. Breen was after him for revenge—and Breen wouldn't stop at anything . . . blackmail, a frameup . . . or murder.

DAY OF THE COMANCHEROS
by Steven C. Lawrence

Their very name struck terror into men's hearts—the Comancheros, a savage army of cutthroats who swept across Texas, leaving behind a bloodstained trail of robbery and murder.